Omensford Series – Book 3

# Donkeys & Demons

G Clatworthy

ISBN: 978-1-915516-19-0

© Gemma Clatworthy 2023

Find more at www.gemmaclatworthy.com

The moral right of Gemma Clatworthy to be identified as the author of this work has been asserted in accordance with the Copyright, Designs and Patents Act of 1988. All rights reserved. No part of this publication may be reproduced, stored in a retrieval system or transmitted in any form or by any means, electronic, mechanical, photocopying, recording or otherwise, without the prior permission of the copyright owner of this book.

This is a work of fiction. All characters and events portrayed in this book are fictional and any resemblance to real people or incidents is purely coincidental.

Cover art by GetCovers.

# Foreword

The Omensford witches first arrived in my writing in [Attack on Avalon](#) (book 5 in the Rise of the Dragons series), but they were too interesting to leave there so they had to have their own series. So, this series was born, based around the fictional town of Omensford in the Cotswolds and the witches who live there.

A special thank you to my amazing typo hunters, grammar gurus, and plot pickers who got this story to where it is today. You are awesome!

If you want to support Gemma, you can find her on [www.patreon.com/G_Clatworthy](http://www.patreon.com/G_Clatworthy) for exclusive first reads of new stories. You can also join her newsletter at [www.gemmaclatworthy.com](http://www.gemmaclatworthy.com) for a free short story based on one of the witches in the Omensford series and follow Gemma on [www.instagram.com/gemmaclatworthy](http://www.instagram.com/gemmaclatworthy), [www.facebook.com/gemmaclatworthy](http://www.facebook.com/gemmaclatworthy) or join the reader's group on Facebook: [Gemma's book wyrms.](#)

## Chapter 1

*Remind me again why I'm coming with you?* the small golden wyrm spoke inside Fi's mind.

"Because you're an awesome familiar, and I don't want to face a horde of small children on my own."

The wyrm snorted, but she climbed up the witch and nestled around her neck.

"Has anyone ever told you that it's too hot for a lizard scarf in July?"

*Has anyone ever told you that it's not a good idea to tease a creature that can breathe fire?*

"Touché," Fi muttered. She glanced in the mirror one last time before heading downstairs.

Her mother and elder sister sat at the large wooden kitchen table, glasses of cool homemade lemonade in their hands. Her niece sat to one side, sketching on white paper with her felt-tip pens.

Agatha stood as Fi entered the room. "Thanks so much for taking Bea to Magic Club today; she's really looking forward to it, aren't you darling?"

On cue, Bea jumped up and ran over to hug her aunt. "Thanks, Aunty Fi."

Fi smiled, unable to resist the childish charms of her niece.

"Hadn't you better get a move on? You don't want to be late." Nell looked pointedly at the cat-shaped kitchen clock.

"We've got plenty of time, Mum."

Bea hopped from foot to foot as Fi poured herself some of the sharp, cloudy lemonade.

"Oh, this came today." Nell held up a postcard with one manicured hand. Fi took it and scanned the spidery handwriting.

*Enjoying being back on the riviera. Not quite as nice as I remember, but then there aren't any Viscounts here this week. Still, I've met a nice young man who says he owns a tech company. Good luck with your presentation. Ciao, Effie x*

Fi flipped it over and smiled at the picture on the front, nonplussed at Effie's knowledge of her presentation; it came with the territory when you were friends with a psychic. If the sunshine yellow beaches, azure skies and tanned, toned bodies on the postcard were anything to go by, Effie was making the most of her second bloom of youth.

"Come on, Aunty Fi!"

"Calm down! It's not as if they're going to start without me; I'm your guest speaker."

Bea headed outside to wait. Fi rolled her eyes. "Remind me again why I agreed to do this?" she muttered.

"Because you're a brilliant aunt who loves their niece, and it gives me and Mum time to finalise plans for the Donkey Derby."

Bea ran back in. "Come on!"

"Alright, alright!" Fi downed the glass and immediately regretted it. Her stomach roiled at the cold liquid. She grabbed her trusty, ancient laptop, safely stowed in its padded bag. It was the only bit of tech that had lasted through her unreliable magical surges, and she'd modified it, so it ran the latest software. At least all she had to do tonight was skip through some slides and hope the flashy animations distracted the kids. Fi took a deep breath and allowed her niece to drag her out of the door.

She almost walked straight into a warlock in a summer dress patterned with frogs.

"Hi, Sita."

"Not at the planning meeting?"

"Not tonight."

"Lucky."

Fi smiled. Her mother was obsessed with the Donkey Derby and the planning meeting was likely a front to make others from the Witches', Wizards' and Warlocks' Institute think they'd had a say. Fi dodged to avoid a wizard levitating a paper fan near their neck and got through the garden gate without crashing into anyone while Bea flitted among the adults, her eyes shining with excitement.

As they walked the short distance to the Omensford village hall, Fi reflected that offering to help her sister out was what had got her into this mess in the first place.

If she hadn't agreed to take Bea to her club last week so Agatha and Neville could have a date night, the leader would never have asked her what she did for a living. Fi had instantly regretted her boast about being a Magical Liaison Office community agent. But it was too late. The leader's eyes had lit up and somehow Fi had agreed to talk to the group of children about what the Office did and why it was important.

It wasn't even like she could share anything exciting. She hadn't done anything significant in her new role. The call about a chimera sighting had turned out to be a large house cat stuck in a bush. And she hadn't made any progress on reports of an enormous pumpkin roaming around local fields. She was ninety-five percent certain it was the same pumpkin that she and Agatha had somehow animated at Halloween, but it wasn't dangerous. After all, come on, what could a giant pumpkin do? Roll over a fence panel?

She gave herself some credit; she had supervised the local solstice celebrations at the nearby stone circle. Not Stonehenge – that was for the real agents – but the smaller circle in the Cotswolds.

But telling some enthusiastic naturist witches and wizards to put some clothes on wasn't exactly hardcore Magical Liaison Office work, or something she could share with primary school kids. It hadn't even shown up on the intra office email roundup. That gave progress updates on the 'proper' missions. Like the agents who had stopped a rogue unicorn from goring pupils in a Scottish school. She sighed. She hadn't even completed the training yet.

They took a shortcut across the local common. In a week, it would be transformed into the site of the Donkey Derby, but for now it was a simple field of grass, made a dry yellow by the summer heat. Two boys ran across the field, kicking a ball between them. Their father traipsed after them.

Bea called out their names in recognition and raced ahead to join the game as Fi sighed again. Great. Now she'd have to talk to the dad. She adjusted her path so they met and did the small, awkward half-smile that all adults have when forced to talk to someone they don't know because their kids are friends.

They had got past the 'hellos' and introductions when a shriek sounded from a nearby garden. Fi stopped, then took a step towards the fence, wondering if someone was hurt. The dad groaned and adjusted his glasses.

"I've told you about playing ball games on the common! It's not allowed! Knock it off!" A shrivelled old lady waved a cane at the children.

Fi frowned. "It's not illegal to kick a ball, is it?"

She instantly regretted opening her mouth. The old woman turned to her, gripping her parrot-headed cane tightly.

"It's a bloody nuisance is what it is! They come here at all hours, day and night, screaming and kicking their balls against my fence. I'll report you! You hear me, you little ruffians? I'll report you! And don't think I don't see you cowering there, Finley, I know what your boys did last weekend. And who are

5

you to tell me what's illegal or not, missy?" The woman punctuated her words by hitting the cane on her fence.

"Er, I'm a community agent for the Magical Liaison Office." Once again, Fi wished she'd kept quiet.

"Oh, are you now? Well, in that case, I'll make a formal report to you right now!"

Fi held her hands up. "Slow down. I only get involved with supernatural cases; these are just some kids kicking a ball around."

The woman looked Fi up and down, taking in her scruffy jeans, stained converse trainers and the vest top with a gaming logo on it – Fi's only concession to the heat.

"So, you won't help me? Figures. Then I'll have to call the police on these hoodlums!"

"OK, OK, we're going, alright? Come on, kids." Fi ushered them to the cut-through on the other side. The woman continued to shout as they left the field.

"You haven't met looney Lucille before?" Finley asked. Fi shook her head. He chuckled. "She's a real piece of work. I don't know why she doesn't move if she hates kids so much. Where does she expect them to play?" He shook his head at the woman's foolishness.

"I suppose there's nowhere for her to go."

"All I know is that it would be better for the village if she left for good."

Fi gave a half smile back then forgot about the incident on the common as the hall loomed ahead. She gulped and gripped her laptop bag to her chest. What was she doing? She wasn't qualified for this.

Bea tugged her hand as they approached the hall. "I can't wait for everyone to meet you!"

At least someone thought she was a hero.

"And Cressida! No one believed me when I said you had a wyrm for a familiar."

Or not. The wyrm around her neck preened itself at Bea's statement.

*I'm ready for my spot in the limelight.*

## Chapter 2

Fi took a deep breath and followed her niece through the swinging doors. Noise assaulted her ears the second she entered. Children. Hundreds of children dashing back and forth around the hall in utter chaos. And all of them screaming at full volume.

Fi winced and shrank back. Cressida hunched her neck in and forced her head into Fi's vest top.

"It's a bit much the first time, isn't it? Don't worry, they'll soon calm down." Fi looked up into the cheery face of their leader. She thrust a hand out and Fi shook it weakly. Fi nodded. It was all she could do. The woman's cheeriness extended to her clothes: bright yellow cut off trousers clashed with a collared shirt in black and white that had the magic club logo printed on it. She topped it off with a pink top hat sat at a jaunty angle on her smoothed back hair. A thin chain around her neck had a pendant that reminded Fi of the Triforce in the Zelda games but with more angles and strange whorls as it jangled over her shirt and the woman tucked it away with a smile as she noticed Fi's eyes on it.

"How would you like me to introduce you?"

"Uh, Fi is fine. And you are?"

The leader giggled. "Well, the kids all call me White Rabbit, but my name's Valerie, Valerie Blanc."

Fi forced her lips up into something that might pass for a smile. On a zombie. There was no way she could meet Valerie's enthusiasm.

"And where can I plug in my laptop for the presentation?" Fi gestured at the padded bag slung over her shoulder.

"Oh, sorry, but the projector screen's stuck. I'm sure it'll be fine if you just talk to them. They're so excited to hear from a real Magical Liaison Office agent!"

Fi swallowed hard. She gripped the shoulder strap tightly. She'd been counting on her slides – with many video excerpts – to get her through this nightmare. Now she had to talk to the children. Her power seeped through her skin in response to her fear.

*That tickles!*

Fi swore under her breath and reigned in her electricity. What was the point of being a tech witch if you couldn't rely on tech?

"If you'll excuse me." Valerie stepped forward, clapped her hands together, and shouted, "All cards in suits!"

The children ran forward and arranged themselves quietly into four neat lines of six. Not hundreds of children then, only twenty-four of them. Cressida peeked out from under Fi's shirt.

*I've changed my mind.*

"Don't even think about it, you're staying!" Fi hissed out of the corner of her mouth.

Cressida prepared to jump down.

"If you stay, I'll buy you steak for a week."

*A month.*

"Deal."

Cressida grinned in a dragonish way and settled back around Fi's shoulders.

"OK cards, first up, I want to say congratulations to those of you who earned the Guardian badge last week, sometimes the greatest magic in the world is looking out for others." Valerie moved between the four rows and handed out round badges embroidered with a hand. "A big cheer for our super magic guardians!"

The children erupted into wild cheers and Fi clapped along, not really sure what was going on.

Valerie held up her hand and the cheering stopped. "Now, we've got a very special guest with us today. Fi is a Magical Liaison Office agent, and she's going to talk to us about her job while I make us some drinks."

Fi stepped forward to the front of the hall with a half wave. Forty-eight keen eyes stared back at her.

"Suits, spread deck!"

On cue, the children arranged themselves in a neat semicircle and sat down. They blinked up at Fi. Bea gave her aunt a thumbs up. A bead of sweat ran down Fi's forehead.

"OK, so I work with the Magical Liaison Office, or the MLO, or Office, as we like to call it, as a community agent."

"Is that like a real agent?"

Fi felt her power shift under her skin. The lights flickered in response to her electrical pull. She took a deep breath and forced her power back under control. The last thing she needed was to blow a fuse in the village hall, or, worse, hurt one of the kids with her wild electric magic.

"Now, Kyle, we put our hands up when we want to ask a question," Valerie admonished the child gently from the kitchen.

Kyle's hand shot up. "Is that like a real agent?"

Fi forced a smile. "Well, a community agent is the representative of the Office in the community. And as Omensford is a protected magical area, you've got your own agent – me!" Fi paused for a laugh. It didn't come. Twenty-four pairs of eyes gazed at her. Fi would have said she had their complete attention, but the children's eyes held a glassy, unfocused look that she put down to boredom. She coughed. "So, if you've got any supernatural problems or you spot anything unusual, you can come to me."

There was silence for a full minute. Fi pulled on her vest. What to do now? Had she bored them all into a catatonic state? She coughed again. When was Valerie coming back? How long did it take to make drinks?

"Er, and before I was a community agent, I worked in IT."

*Brilliant. Really interesting topic.*

"Er, and I dealt with a chimera sighting the other week. It turned out to be Mrs Muggins' cat, but I had to shut the High Street for an afternoon."

All the children snapped back to attention, as if a switch had flicked back on. Hands waved. Fi pointed to a child at random.

"Yes, do you have a question?"

"But what exactly do you do?"

"Uh, I supervise local magical events, like the solstice celebrations. And if there's anything unusual, you can report it on our website, or to me directly, I suppose, and I look into it."

"My gran was at the Cotswold stone circle; she said you ruined the solstice!"

"How many missions have you been on?"

"Can we see your weapons?"

"Have you fought any monsters?"

"Can I stroke your wyrm?"

Fi's throat seized up and sweat gathered in the small of her back.

"Children! One at a time, give Fi a chance to answer your questions." Valerie smiled encouragingly at Fi as she bustled into the room with a tray of drinks. Fi took the offered drink and sipped slowly, drawing out the time before she had to answer while Valerie placed the tray down on a table and began unloading the plastic cups.

"Uh, well, I haven't exactly been on any missions yet, per se, but I have investigated a few things. I don't have a weapon, and the MLO's job isn't to fight monsters, it's to make sure that the supernatural has a positive impact on people's lives." That wasn't strictly true. The Office helped to manage the tension between mundane and magical beings. Sometimes that meant fighting monsters. But that wasn't what they told the public, let alone a group of fidgeting children. "And yes! Her name is Cressida, and she loves being tickled under the chin!"

*What?!*

"Sorry," Fi whispered as she grasped firmly and dislodged the wyrm from her spot on Fi's shoulders and put her on the ground. The children swarmed round and petted the dragon-like creature.

*Steak for two months…oh, yes, right there…*

Fi smiled to herself.

"You did great! Thanks for coming; the children are so curious," Valerie said, standing next to the witch and beaming at the crowd of kids surrounding the wyrm.

Fi murmured her agreement, privately thinking that it could hardly have gone worse.

"Will you stay for the games?"

Fi thought of a hundred reasons why she had to leave, but the lies died on her lips, and she found herself agreeing. The children spent the remainder of the hour running round and generally wearing themselves out while shouting. Continuously. There was some sort of order to the games but after a soft, sponge ball collided with the back of her head, Fi watched from the side-lines.

After the longest sixty minutes of Fi's life, Valerie clapped her hands and got the kids to line up again. "Alright cards, give a big thank you and our magic club salute to our special guest – Fi!"

The children turned to Fi and, with a flourish, waved imaginary magic wands in the air before pointing them at the witch. Fi did a small half bow.

"And now, cards, let's shuffle out and play parent snap." Valerie opened the hall doors and waved each child out to their waiting adults. Bea ran over to Fi.

"Did you see their faces when they saw Cressida?!"

## Chapter 3

Fi walked home in silence as Bea chattered about their evening. At least her niece had enjoyed it. It had felt like a disaster to her. She should never have agreed to speak. As they approached her childhood home, Fi wished she had a proper investigation she could have shared with the kids. She huffed annoyed that she still sought approval from kids; hadn't she grown out of that now she didn't have to face the constant teasing of the schoolyard.

Her mind flashed back to her schooldays and her early obsession with technology. Computers weren't considered that cool in the nineties – nerdy, but not cool – and she hadn't connected with any of her schoolmates. She shook her head against the dark thoughts on a summer's day. At least the friends she'd made online helped fill the well of loneliness she'd had as a teenager. She was still in touch with five of them today and her lips curved up as she remembered their most recent gaming session where they'd trounced a group of teenagers in a battlefield brawl.

"Cressida was so cool." Bea's voice brought her back to the present.

*I do my best.*

"She says thank you," Fi said and Bea grinned and reached up to tickle Cressida's tail.

They ambled through the garden, enjoying the warm summer's evening. It was sweltering during the day in the heatwave, but it cooled to a bearable temperature once the sun retreated beneath the horizon. The flowers swayed in a soft breeze as they passed, sending waves of lavender around them.

As they neared the door, it swung open, and Fi gave the door frame a friendly pat as they walked inside.

Nell looked up from the stack of papers in front of her. "How was it?"

Fi grimaced but Bea plonked herself on a chair, pushed aside a detailed map of the common that showed every bump in the field and answered. "It was great! Everyone believes me about Cressida now and Aunty Fi was awesome, plus we got to play ladders!" She paused to draw a breath.

"Wow, sounds like you had a great time." Agatha stood and shut the bound diary with a snap. "We'd better be getting home; I think we're done for tonight."

"Alright," Nell said, "but remember we still need to agree on where to put the ducking stool."

"We'll sort it tomorrow. Come on, Bea, say thank you to your aunt."

"Thanks, Aunty Fi." Bea gave her a quick hug before grabbing her drawings and scurrying after her mother. Fi and Nell gave them a wave as they took to their skies on Agatha's broomstick.

"Sounds like you were brilliant." Nell smiled at her youngest daughter.

"Um, no. It was awful, but it's over now." Fi sighed and changed the subject. "How was the planning meeting?"

"Oh, it went well but the temperature's set to be over thirty degrees so there's lots of debate about the best way to keep everyone cool and whether we can even have the donkey races."

"Can't you conjure up some cool weather?"

Nell gave her daughter a look. "Of course we could, it's just whether that's the best thing to do. Weather spells can be temperamental –"

"You mean, temperature-mental!"

Nell raised an eyebrow at the bad pun but didn't comment. "As I was saying, it can be difficult to predict the outcome of weather spells in extreme conditions, like this heatwave, so not everyone's convinced it's the right thing to do. I wish Effie was here, she'd be able to predict if the heat is going to continue."

It was Fi's turn to give her mother a look. "You wish Effie were here instead of travelling the world?"

Her mother sighed. "Of course, I want her to enjoy her second lease of life. But her predictions are always so accurate."

Fi nodded in agreement. Effie was the best psychic they knew, but after her soul had been transferred into a younger body, she had abandoned village life for something far more exotic. Fi's phone buzzed. She glanced down at the screen automatically. Then did a double take. It was the Magical Liaison Office. There had been an incident.

## Chapter 4

Fi's first thought on seeing the dead body was that there were some things that eyes were not meant to see. Her second thought was: be careful what you wish for. She'd been excited to receive the text, after she'd double checked it wasn't some silly prank from Maxi, her friend at the Office and tech enthusiast.

Now she struggled to keep her lemonade down as she surveyed the scene. She averted her gaze and asked Detective Ledd to repeat himself feeling her blood sink to her feet as she swayed, overcome by a sudden surge of dizziness.

The detective led her away to the edge of the common. Considering a few months ago, he'd wanted to arrest her for murder, his sympathy came as a surprise. "You never get used to it, you know."

"What?"

"Seeing a dead body."

Fi nodded. She'd walked past these trees earlier this evening on the way back from the magic club. Maybe the body had already been there, or maybe the murderer had killed them while she walked past chatting to her niece...she shuddered. When she'd accepted the job with the Office, she hadn't expected dead bodies. She'd wanted problems to solve and a purpose, but honestly, the only blood she could stomach was the fake kind on the online games she played.

Not that blood was an issue here. As the detective repeated.

"A dog walker found the body inside the treeline about an hour ago. We're still working on identifying the body, but it's an elderly person; grey hair, cardigan. We think it's a woman, but it could be a bloke with long hair. I've left it to the Doc to check. We don't know exactly how old because the body's drained of blood and dried out. To be honest, when Constable Beckett called it in, I thought it was a hoax."

Fi could see why. The body resembled a mummified corpse, like the kind you can see in museums, preserved for thousands of years in airtight tombs. It was easy to think it was a prank. Someone could have got hold of an ancient body and dressed it in modern clothes... Fi clutched onto that theory.

"The Doc's looking at her now to get a time of death, but the method is clear. Someone slit their throat. But – and this is the reason I called it in with the magic people – there's no blood. So, assuming this isn't some sort of joke, I reckon something supernatural is going on."

He looked pleased with himself at that assessment and Fi nodded along, ignoring her roiling stomach. She took a deep breath and indicated that she was ready to have another look. The detective squinted at her, then came to some sort of conclusion and nodded curtly. He headed back to the roped off part of the field. Fi followed.

The doctor stood, wiping his hands on his cargo shorts. Fi gave a start of surprise. She'd been too focused on the disturbing body with its shrivelled skin to notice that the doctor was Mort. Of course it was. Who else would it be?

His tone was professional. "No other injuries that I can see here, so I'd say the wound in her throat is the cause of death."

"Her?"

"I checked; the victim is female. I've contacted the coroner; she'll look at her in the morning. Until then, I've asked for transport to the morgue. They're waiting over there..." The detective nodded. This must be normal procedure. "Unless there's anything you want to do?"

Fi started. "What?"

"Is there anything you need to do?"

"With the body?!"

"To see if it's something supernatural?"

"Oh. Right." Fi had no idea what to do. She closed her eyes and concentrated. Nothing. She couldn't feel any spark of magic. But there were lots of ways to kill someone that didn't use magic. Cressida climbed down from her spot on Fi's shoulders.

"Should that creature be here?" Detective Ledd asked with a frown.

"She's, uh, a special crime scene wyrm," Fi lied.

"Well, she'd better not disturb the scene."

What scene? she thought. There was the corpse, but no blood, no footprints in the dry grass. No helpful clues like a confession from the killer stapled to the body. Nothing. Fi's eyes tracked the golden wyrm as she sniffed the body delicately, then moved to a spot across the field. The witch repressed a shudder. What if the killer had chosen her or, worse, Bea as they walked home?

*Brimstone.*

"What?"

*Brimstone. Sulphur. Can't you smell it?*

Fi sniffed the air and shook her head.

*It's strongest here.*

"Has she found something?"

Fi ignored the question and joined Cressida. She bent down. Was it her imagination, or was there the slightest hint of burning? She got out her phone and shone the built-in torch at the ground. A patch of grass was burned black.

"Here!" she shouted. The detective and the doctor ran over.

Detective Ledd pursed his lips. "A bit of burned grass? This could be anything. Most likely kids having a barbeque."

Fi shook her head. "It's important."

"Alright," said the detective in tones that clearly suggested he disagreed. But to his credit, he called over a scene of crime officer and had them take pictures.

"Anything else, or can we release the corpse?"

"No, that's all." Fi tried to channel her mother's tone. It must not have worked, because the detective raised one bushy eyebrow at her, making him look like he was having a stroke, and then headed off to inform the people waiting at the edge of the field that they could take the body away.

Fi huffed out a sigh, unsure what the protocol was for leaving a crime scene.

"Look, I know this isn't the right time, but can we talk?" Mort asked.

## Chapter 5

Fi stared at Mort. He twisted his hands nervously as he waited for her response. She'd known this was coming. She'd avoided him ever since the Spring Social. No easy feat in a small community.

"Er..."

"I know I'm asking a lot, but I'd really like to talk."

"OK," Fi said. She could at least give him that.

He gestured to a bench set up under towering trees that rustled gently in the light breeze. Fi kicked away an empty glass bottle, the remnants of teenage hijinks. Fi wrinkled her nose. She'd never been invited to any of those drinking sessions unless Agatha had let her tag along. Her memories of sipping cheap cider in the park or on the common on hazy summer's evenings were tinged with feeling like she didn't belong or that she'd rather be in a chatroom with her real friends.

They sat down together. Fi was careful to make sure there was a clear gap between them, even as her heart raced at his proximity.

"So…"

"So…" she echoed back. What was there to say? She'd panicked the morning after waking up in his bed. Then she'd fled while he was making breakfast. A really mature move.

"The Spring Social, it meant a lot to me…" Mort started. Fi nodded, not meeting his eyes. He rubbed the back of his neck in frustration. "I understand if you want to be friends, but I wanted you to know that…it meant something…to me."

Fi stared at her shoes as she scuffed the grass by her feet. What was she meant to say to that? Trust sexy doctor Mort to be perfectly happy talking about his feelings. As the silence stretched on, he sighed and stood.

"OK, well, see you around, Fi."

"It meant something to me, too." Her voice was quiet, barely above a whisper, but he turned. His brown eyes searched her face.

"Then what's the problem? Why have you been avoiding me?"

"I don't know."

He looked up at the branches above them as if an answer might fall from the sky. "What does that mean?"

"I don't know."

*You do,* Cressida's voice hissed through her mind.

"Do you want to be with me?"

25

"I don't not want to be with you."

*What does that mean?*

Mort threw up his hands. "That's not an answer!" He thought for a moment. "Does this have something to do with that chap you were talking to?"

Fi screwed up her face as she thought back to the dance. "Maxi?"

"So, it is something to do with him."

Fi jumped to her feet. "No! No, we're just friends."

"Then what, Fi?" Mort brought his hand up to tuck a strand of hair behind her ear, but stopped himself and lowered his arm with a sigh.

"I don't jump into bed with people after one date. That's not who I am—"

"I never said it was!"

"You might be comfortable with one-night stands, but—"

"Is that what you think? That I wanted a one-night stand? I see." Mort nodded to himself, his lips tight before he turned back to Fi. "I'll see you around, Fi."

He stalked off, got three paces away then whirled back. "And for what it's worth, I've never even had a one-night stand. You didn't stick around but we were both drunk. We never... we just slept."

Fi hugged her arms around her chest, unsure if it was relief or embarrassment that heated her heart. "Look, I'm not good at this relationship stuff, OK?"

Mort sighed and raked his hand through his black hair. "You didn't even give us a chance to get to the relationship part."

"I know."

He waited for her to say something more. She carried on staring at her feet, studying the pattern on her converse trainers. She wanted to tell him that she'd end up hurting him, but her mouth didn't seem to be working.

"So, what do you want?"

"I don't know."

"OK, well, when you figure it out, I'm ready to talk." He sighed and walked away, his shoulders slumped.

Fi turned and walked in the opposite direction. Her power swirled under her skin as her emotions bubbled up. She felt her hair rise as her electricity mounted. She sniffed and wiped her nose with the back of her hand. Fi forced down her power before she fried her phone. She was not going to cry. Nope, she was going to do the mature thing and run home to her room.

*You really messed that up. Why not tell him that you like him?*

"It's not that simple. I don't know how I feel."

*It's obvious to anyone, even with your inferior senses.*

Fi opened her mouth to say something sarcastic back to the wyrm, when her legs tangled in something, and she fell to the ground.

At the sound of the tumble, Mort hurried over and offered her his hand. As Mort helped her up, she kicked the offending trip hazard and froze as a polished wooden parrot glinted in the lazy moonlight. She knew who the victim was.

## Chapter 6

News spread fast in Omensford. First thing the following morning, as Fi ate a piece of toast with marmalade and considered her black coffee – Goblin Blend, extra strong – Agatha walked through the door with Bea in tow.

"I can't believe it!"

Fi raised her eyebrows in an unspoken question.

"Lucille Dankworth. Dead!"

Fi looked pointedly from Agatha to Bea. Bea answered with the precociousness of all seven-year-olds as she stifled a yawn. "I don't mind. She was a mean lady. Now we'll be able to play football on the common."

"Beatrice Blair! Don't speak ill of the dead!" Agatha made a sign, clenching her fist and poking her thumb between her middle and index fingers as she made a small circle over her heart to ward against evil spirits. "Go do some drawing while I talk with your aunt."

Bea set up her pad of paper and pencils on the table, her head drooping as she doodled. Agatha jerked her head to get Fi to join her in the kitchen area. With a resigned sigh, Fi got up from the table and moved her plate and coffee mug onto the side.

"Aren't you meant to be at work?" she asked Agatha.

"Not for thirty minutes. Sita said Lucille was murdered and they think it's the occult."

"Who thinks what is occult?" Nell swept into the room and gave Bea a kiss before joining her daughters by the stove.

"Someone's killed Lucille Dankworth!"

Nell waved her hand dismissively. "Yes, I heard that on the news."

"Sita said they think it's an occult killing."

"How would Sita know?"

Agatha shrugged.

"You were called out last night, Fi. Was that the incident?"

Fi sniffed. "I can't talk about an ongoing investigation." There. That sounded nice and official.

"That's a yes. So, was it murder?"

"I'm not going to talk about it!"

"Alright, alright," Agatha held up her hands in a pacifying manner. "But what are you going to do next?"

"What?"

"You're on the investigation, right?"

"Oh...yes, of course. Well, I'll probably join Detective Ledd as he does the rounds of her friends and family."

"Who were her friends? She was a nasty piece of work from everything I've heard."

"What did you say to Bea about speaking ill of the dead?"

Nell interrupted the bickering. "She wasn't WWWI, of course. I heard she was down the pub often enough. I'd start there."

"Just because she wasn't part of the Witches', Wizards' and Warlocks' Institute doesn't mean she was a bad person, Mum."

Nell sniffed in response.

Agatha glanced at the cat-shaped kitchen clock and gasped. "Come on, Bea! We've got to go, or we'll be late!"

"I don't want to go..." The child had dark smudges under her eyes, and she pulled back as her mother grabbed for her hand. "Please, Mum, I'm tired and Mr Hackett is horrible!"

"Bea! I don't want to hear it."

"But he is! All the kids hate him, and yesterday, he threw a dodgeball at Kyle! We weren't even playing dodgeball!"

Agatha pursed her lips. "I'll talk to him. Now, come on!"

She threw pens and paper into Bea's schoolbag and raced out of the door to get across the village before the school opened.

"Well?" Nell asked.

"Well, what?"

"Don't you have some investigating to do?"

"Not until I've finished my coffee."

## Chapter 7

Once she'd finished her breakfast, Fi contacted Detective Ledd. He wasn't happy about her tagging along, but identification had confirmed that the dead body was indeed Lucille Dankworth, so supernatural causes were very much in play; and that meant the Magical Liaison Office was involved.

The coroner's exam was scheduled for nine thirty a.m. in the local morgue. Local being a relative term as the morgue was set up near Magewell and covered several local villages in the Cotswolds. Fi had asked about bus routes. Detective Ledd hadn't sworn but he had taken a deep breath and offered Fi a lift; as long as she didn't bring the wyrm.

So, here she was; in the detective's small Fiat, pootling towards the morgue. He drove slowly along the country lanes, with strains of classical music playing through the radio. The soothing violins were interrupted only by the news; the headline was on the heatwave – today was set to be another scorcher, followed by reports that supernaturals, and dragons in particular, were to blame. Fi shook her head in silent frustration. Anything to distract from humanity's contribution to climate change.

Without any conversation, her mind turned to Mort. What did she want? She enjoyed being around him, but any time she got close to someone, she hurt them. Either with her power or because she couldn't commit – not the way normal people did anyway. And they'd had a one-night stand! Except they had just slept together, did that make it more or less intimate?

"First time?"

"What?" Fi choked on her own tongue. Why was Detective Ledd asking about her sex life? That wasn't his business.

"At an autopsy?"

Fi turned away from the yellowed fields rolling past the window and took a deep breath. A perfectly acceptable work-related question. She nodded. "What should I expect?"

Detective Ledd snorted. "Well, it's not like it is on TV. They can't get the smell across on screen. And if you're squeamish, you might as well wait outside."

Fi resolved that she would stay in the room whatever happened. They travelled the rest of the way in silence, Fi's fingers tapping against her thigh as they wound through the countryside towards the morgue, and her nerves mounted. At this point, the interminable journey was worse than anything the coroner could do.

She wanted to scream at the detective to overtake a slow-moving tractor and get a move on, but instead she bit the inside of her mouth and kept quiet.

The car pulled up on the gravelled drive one minute before the appointed examination time. The detective sprung out of the car and slammed the door shut behind him. Fi joined him outside, the growing heat surrounding her like an oven. Her feet crunched on the stones as they headed for the morgue, sweat clinging to her skin despite the short walk.

As Fi stepped through the automatic doors, she heaved a sigh of pleasure. Air conditioning. The detective signed them in with the receptionist who waved them through. Fi breathed in the smell as they headed deeper into the morgue; chemicals, disinfectant, bleach and something sickly sweet and rotting underneath it all. Detective Ledd had been right; that odour didn't come across in the detective shows that she watched with Cressida.

She steeled herself and followed the detective through a set of doors into an operating room. The temperature was even lower in here and the hairs on Fi's arms rose in goose pimples at the chill. The room was lined with neat, white tiles; easy to wipe down, she thought. There was a row of cupboards along one wall. A fridge was marked with signs for dangerous chemicals and a metal gurney sat in the centre of the room with a smaller silver table next to it that held wickedly sharp medical instruments.

Next to the metal gurney was a woman with a crisp fringe over her severe face. She peered over her pointed, straight nose at them and adjusted her glasses.

"You're late."

Fi's eyes flicked to the round clock on the wall. It was nine thirty-one a.m.

Detective Ledd smiled and ignored the comment. "Ready when you are, Robbie."

Her piercing black eyes took in Fi. "Who's the newbie?"

"Magical Liaison Office."

Robbie grunted and took out a digital recorder. She pressed play and placed it next to the sharp implements on the table. She noted the date, time, her name and the detective's name, before looking to Fi.

"Also present is…"

"Fi, uh, Fiona Blair, Magical Liaison Office."

Robbie continued by stating Lucille's name and then listing everything she noticed about the outside of the body, including the deep cut across her throat. The coroner exchanged her glasses for magnifying lenses and bent over the wound, opening it slightly with a scalpel to see if there was anything inside. Fi stared at a spot on Lucille's shrivelled hand to avoid looking at the gash.

"Wound is slightly deeper on the left-hand side, suggesting that either the killer was left-handed and facing the victim, or, more likely, the killer was able to attack from behind in which case we're looking for a right-handed killer. Nothing left in the wound. The cut was made with a sharp tool, with a straight blade, possibly a knife."

"Would you expect a lot of blood from a wound like that?" Fi asked, unable to tear her eyes from the corpse.

The coroner lifted her head, her dark eyes glittered like beetles behind her lenses. "Normally, yes. I'd expect blood around the wound and more blood down the skin, on the clothes, on the ground where she was found. But there's no bloodstains on the body. So, possibly she was moved. However, the real puzzle is the complete lack of blood anywhere *in* her body. Total exsanguination is very unusual."

"How unusual?"

She met Fi's gaze. "I've never seen it before." She paused then gave a smile, "But, it does mean that everything inside will be well preserved, so let's have a look."

Robbie selected a sharp instrument and began methodically cutting into the corpse. The sickly-sweet smell that permeated the room intensified, mixed with a dusty aroma, like paper left for too long. Fi flinched, expecting blood to pour out. Of course, it didn't. She wanted to tear her gaze away, but her eyes remained fixed on the body. It was like watching a horror film, even though you know it's going to end badly, you can't stop look away.

There was no blood oozing from the cuts though. One of the benefits of the body being drained dry. And Fi found she could watch if she imagined it was an ancient iron age body instead of a villager she had seen alive only yesterday. Robbie kept the commentary going as she removed desiccated organs and placed samples into pots for further analysis.

After two hours, the coroner stopped. She removed the rubber gloves that fitted over her small hands like a second skin and walked to the metal sink to scrub up.

"The most likely cause of death is the wound to the neck. Other than that, and her age, she's in good shape…but the lack of blood…well, it's got me puzzled."

"And time of death?" Detective Ledd pushed.

"Hard to tell as there's none of the usual signs we look for, but given the eyewitness sightings, and the time of discovery…" Robbie checked the report. "I'd say between seven and eight-thirty p.m."

The detective grunted and made a note in his leather-bound book. Fi made her own note on her phone.

"I need a coffee before I sew her up. Fancy joining me?"

## Chapter 8

Robbie led the way through the morgue to a small room with a couple of low chairs upholstered in an institutional orange colour that was probably meant to be uplifting but read more like depressed seventies styling.

She boiled the kettle and offered tea or coffee.

"Coffee, black, please. Two sugars."

"It's instant."

Fi nodded and sank into one of the hideous square chairs. As long as it contained caffeine, she would be happy.

Detective Ledd preferred a strong, milky tea and made his own in a plain, white mug as Robbie sorted two coffees.

They drank in silence.

"So, what do you think it is?"

Fi nearly spilled the coffee when she realised the question was directed at her. "Er, I wouldn't like to say. How could you drain the blood so completely that a body becomes a dried husk?"

"How would I do it?" Robbie considered for a minute. "Well, it would be difficult. Obviously, you could slit the throat and hang them upside down and catch all the blood in some sort of container. I think that would be messy though, and you'd need a big container for 10-11 pints of blood...

"The best way would be to hook an artery up to a tube and drain it out. But that would take time, and there'd be a hole in the body and no need to cut the throat…"

Fi stared, her coffee forgotten. "Remind me never to get on your bad side."

Robbie flashed her a smile. "It's a hazard of the job. You see so much death, it becomes second nature. I forgot you were new to this. You held up really well in there. I've had six-foot-tall officers come in and faint at the first incision."

Pride flooded through Fi's chest.

"Anyway, neither of those methods would cause the drying we saw on Lucille. If I didn't know she'd been killed yesterday, I would have thought Larry here was having me on with a body from a museum."

Larry snorted. "That's exactly what I thought when I saw her, probably would still think that if Fiona hadn't tripped over her cane."

The coroner took another sip of tea and stared at a point on the white wall. "Of course, the real question is; what did they do with all the blood?"

She came out of her reverie and noticed them staring at her. Robbie shrugged. "Well, it's gone somewhere, it hasn't evaporated."

## Chapter 9

Fi and Detective Ledd were quiet on the journey back to Omensford. Robbie had made a good point and it unnerved Fi. She bit her lip as uneasy thoughts swirled in her head. There were some uses for blood in magic, of course. But most spells she knew of required a drop, not an entire body's worth.

Unless it was blood magic. No one in the magical community liked talking about the tainted strand of magic. It wasn't widely practiced and was considered evil. She tried to recall the signs of a blood magician she'd been taught in magic class. It was no good. It was too long ago and, unless computers were involved, she hadn't paid much attention.

"Where do you want me to drop you off?" The detective's voice cut through her thoughts. She focused on the countryside and realised they were entering Omensford.

"Er, what are you doing now? Shouldn't I stay on as part of the investigation?"

Larry huffed a sigh, but he couldn't say no. "Alright. I'm heading over to Lucille's house to take a look around, then I want to talk to the neighbours, see if they heard anything last night."

"Great, I'll come with you."

He grunted and turned the car down the street where Lucille Dankworth had lived. It was a pretty street, with houses made from butter-coloured Cotswold stone and neat gardens hemmed in by trimmed hedges. The detective parked on the street and flicked through his notepad for the house number. Fi wondered why people didn't use their phones instead of paper; it was so much easier to search.

She followed as the detective headed for a house in the middle of the row. He pushed open a low, wooden gate and strode towards the door. Large lavender bushes lined the short, paved path from the road to her front door. Their fragrant scent filled Fi's nose as she brushed against them.

Fi wondered how they would get in. Lucille had lived alone as far as she could see and the detective didn't look like he could break down the door. But, clearly the detective had insights into village life because he lifted the doormat and there was a spare key, shining in the late morning sun. He lifted it triumphantly and fitted it into the lock. It turned easily and he swung the door open.

Before he crossed the threshold, he turned back to Fi and raised one finger in warning. "Stick with me and don't mess around in here; it's a potential crime scene."

Fi rolled her eyes. "I'm not an idiot."

The detective glared at her before heading inside. Fi squared her shoulders and followed. The hallway was dark with patterned wallpaper that added to the closed-in feel.

Fi peeked into the lounge, where Larry had paused. A dull corduroy-clad sofa and armchair faced an old TV. Fi couldn't help it, she stared. It was old enough to have dials and an aerial sticking out of the top. Fi guessed Lucille wasn't the type to stream her television programmes.

Tucked into one corner, a dark-wood display cabinet with glass shelves held a lifetime's worth of knick-knacks. Small porcelain dogs and frogs vied for space with commemorative plates and cups. It was exactly the sort of thing that her mother would hate.

After the detective had studied the Radio Times magazines and faded photographs, he moved to the kitchen. Fi followed. It wasn't like she had any other options in the standard terraced two up-two down house. The kitchen was small and serviceable, this time with Formica clad cupboards and work surfaces. The walls were a faded lime green that somehow leant an air of oppression to the small space, like someone trying too hard to brighten a room had instead sucked any soul out of the place. The one redeeming feature was the large window overlooking the garden.

A dented cardboard box near the door held balls of every shape and size. Fi frowned. She couldn't imagine the old lady playing so many different sports.

Fi tried the back door. It was unlocked. Behind her, Detective Ledd huffed, but he didn't say anything, so Fi went outside. The lawn was neatly trimmed, and a deep green despite the heat. Fi wondered if Lucille had been a witch, before she saw the bright yellow sprinkler. No hose pipe bans for the Dankworth lawn.

Loud laughter assaulted her ears followed by a rhythmic thud. Fi saw an upturned crate by the fence. She stepped onto it and could easily see into the neighbours' gardens. Two children tore up and down the garden chasing a basketball. One of them got it and dribbled it to the patio – that explained the thumping – before taking a shot. It went wide with another thud as the ball bounced off of the back wall and headed for Fi. She ducked.

"Awwww! Now look what you've done!"

"No, I can go and get it!"

"No way! You know what she did to the last kid who stepped on her lawn? She gutted him! The body's still in the cellar."

"She's dead, so it doesn't matter." But the young voice sounded hesitant.

"Her ghost will get you!"

Fi decided it was time to interrupt the scare stories. She retrieved the ball and returned to her spot on the crate. "Looking for this?"

"Who are you?"

"My name's Fiona. I'm with the Magical Liaison Office."

"Throw it back then."

"What can you tell me about your neighbour?"

"Looney Lucille? She was cuckoo, complete nutbar, banana poo, if you know what I mean."

"In what way?"

"She told Mum that we couldn't play in the garden 'cos it was above legal noise levels."

"And she used to steal our balls!"

That explained the box – the old lady was a closet ball thief.

"Yeah," the second kid agreed with a vigorous nod, "if any of our toys went in her garden, she used to cut 'em up with her shears. We saw her do it!"

"And we asked her to stop but she did it anyway, stupid old witch! Oh, sorry."

Fi let the prejudiced comment go. "So, you didn't like her."

"Nope. Can we have our ball back?"

"One more question, did you see anything last night?"

The first kid shook his head. "Nope, we were at the magic club. Hang on, you were there too? Are you investigating the murder? Cool."

The detective spluttered behind her. Fi spoke quickly. "Uh, no, murder is not cool kids. Here's your ball." She aimed for the basketball hoop. It would have been so cool if she'd have got it in, but, naturally, it bounced off the rim and hit one of the plant pots on the patio. Fi gaped as the children's mother ran out.

"Which of you did that to my marigolds?"

"It wasn't us, Mum! It was her!" Twin accusing fingers pointed at the tech witch.

Fi tucked a strand of white hair back behind her ear. "Sorry about that."

But the woman's curiosity outweighed her annoyance at a damaged pot. "Are you here about her murder?"

"We're investigating her death, yes." Detective Ledd forced himself onto the crate next to Fi, his thick fingers gripping the wooden fence for support.

"Well, I'm not surprised someone killed her. She was awful to my kids, and anyone on the common. It was like no one could have any fun without her say so."

"And did anyone dislike her enough to kill her?"

"It wasn't me, if that's what you're thinking. I'll admit sometimes I turned up the TV too loud just to annoy her, but she thumped on the wall with that ugly cane until I turned it back down."

"Did she have any hobbies at all?"

"Other than terrorising the local kids?" The woman thought for a moment. "If you count going down the pub as a hobby. It was the only time my boys could play in the garden when she went down there. I think she was friendly with the landlord, but she was never out past nine o'clock."

"Thank you, that's very helpful, Ms…"

"Chester, Eileen Chester. And don't worry about solving anything too quickly, it's a relief to have her house empty for a change."

Fi hopped down from the crate and walked to the end of the garden. She stood in the same spot where Lucille had threatened them with her cane the night before. She shuddered. It was weird standing where a dead person had stood, not that it should be weird. Dead people had stood just about everywhere, if you went back far enough. Fi screwed up her face as she tried to puzzle out her own thoughts.

The detective joined her. "What are you thinking?"

Fi decided not to share her theory on where deceased people may have stood and instead focused on the murder.

"No blood in the house or garden. Either she was killed somewhere else and dragged to her final resting place after they'd dried her out, or the murderer did everything on the common quick enough not to be noticed."

"Now you're thinking like a detective. We still need to check upstairs, but I think you're right." Fi did a double take. "Unorthodox but right. Oh, and don't talk to any more witnesses without me."

Fi nodded. That was more like the detective that she knew and loved... well... didn't hate.

They checked upstairs but there was nothing of interest. Unless you liked unmade beds and more faded photographs in ugly frames on every available surface. Fi could have sworn a few of them were the prints that came with the frames.

"So, what's next, detective?"

Larry looked at her and took out his notepad. "Pub?"

## Chapter 10

The regulars – Jeremy and Jack – were in their usual spots on the bench outside the local pub; the Witch's Brew. Fi ignored the sign – she was used to the green-skinned witch with the prominent wart on her nose and stereotypical black, pointed hat on her head – and walked past the two old boys. They raised their empty glasses to her in part salutation, part hope that she might fill them with ale.

"Woah! Careful there, sonny!" Harris the farmer stopped short to avoid a collision with the broad detective. "Nearly spilled the pints."

"Sorry," said the detective through clenched teeth.

Still muttering, Harris joined his friends on the wooden bench and passed out amber pints of real ale with half an inch of thick foam topping the drinks.

"You'll be here about Lucille," Jack, or possibly Jeremy, said before he took a long drink.

Detective Ledd paused halfway into the pub.

"Did you know her?" Fi jumped on the tidbit and sat down on a nearby picnic table, selecting a spot in the meagre shade provided by an angled table parasol.

"Aye," replied Harris with a shake of his head. All three men took a drink. The hoppy smell of real ale and sweat clung to them like a cloud in the thick heat.

"And?" Fi prompted when it was clear they weren't going to volunteer any information.

Harris thought a moment and scratched his whiskery chin. "And she could hold her drink, I'll tell you that!"

"Ain't that the truth!"

"For such a small lady, she could match anyone pint for pint."

"Not that she drank pints o'course. She was more of a gin and tonic girl…"

"Hold the tonic!"

The three of them broke out into howls of laughter at the shared jibe. Fi smiled along.

"Aye, she liked the hard stuff."

"As the actress said to the priest!"

More laughter.

"So, was she here yesterday?" Fi pressed on.

Jeremy, or possibly Jack, tilted his head as he considered the question. "No, I don't think as she was here yesterday."

Jack, or maybe Jeremy, nodded and fanned his once white vest top, exposing more of his grey, wiry chest hair. "That's right. Right unusual it were, but then she didn't always make it. Not if there was something on the telly she wanted to watch."

"Like what?"

"Gardener's World or the Bake Off were her favourites and she didn't hold with recording them and watching them back. But she was here most nights."

"Nights?" asked the detective, finally joining the conversation.

"We-ell, evenings. I don't recall as she ever stayed past nine p.m., she was always worried about walking home on her own, although we was always more worried for anyone she met on the way – she couldn't half give you a wallop with that cane!"

"Now, Harris, you deserved that whack."

"Serve you right."

"You mean, she assaulted you?" Detective Ledd scribbled furiously in his notebook.

"No, no, nothing like that detective. Some friendly banter got out of hand is all."

"What he means is, he offered to show her his vegetable and she walloped him!"

"I only wanted to show off my prize-winning parsnip!"

Jack and Jeremy burst into laughter. Fi guffawed – she had seen some of Harris' anatomical vegetables before – then turned her laugh into a spluttering cough as the detective gave her a sharp look. He put his notebook away.

"Here, don't we get something for helping you with your enquiries?"

"It's thirsty work talking about the dead."

Detective Ledd sighed and went inside. Fi drummed her fingers on the table for a minute then asked, "Can you think of anyone who might have wanted her dead?"

The three men went quiet, suddenly more sober than they had appeared.

"Not so much wanted her dead…"

"But there were a few who wouldn't be sorry to see her go…"

"Like who?" Fi leaned forwards.

"Well, she could be a bit hard to take, see, especially if she thought you were winding her up. That's why she hated the local kids on the common, she thought they were out to annoy her."

Fi nodded. That chimed with what she'd experienced and with what the neighbour had said.

"And she had a spot at the bar…" Harris added.

"Oh-ho! Heaven help you if you sat at her spot when she was here!" The men laughed again. It seemed as if the three of them had fond memories of Lucille. From what everyone else had said so far, they might be the only people in Omensford who did.

Detective Ledd returned with three half pints and placed the tray on the table. He made eye contact with Fi, waggled his eyebrows and bobbed his head. Fi frowned before realising that he wanted her to follow him. She said her goodbyes to Harris, Jeremy and Jack and walked with the detective to the village centre.

"Did they tell you anything while I was inside?"

"Not really, just that she had a spot at the bar and hated kids but it doesn't seem reason enough for someone to murder her."

"Don't be so sure. Who knows what evil lurks in the hearts of men. People can do all sorts of horrible things to each other, things you wouldn't believe –"

"How many murders have you investigated?" Fi blurted out her question and interrupted his lecture on the evil of mankind. She instantly regretted it. She'd crossed some sort of social norm, if only there was some guide she could study. There must be a website on it.

Detective Ledd pulled himself up to his full height and met her gaze coldly. "I have led five murder investigations."

"Including this one?"

"Yes." Larry deflated a little. Fi clamped her lips together to avoid saying something else to hurt his feelings, but she'd been involved in at least two of the investigations, three if you counted Lucille.

"Did the landlord tell you anything?" Fi asked after a minute of silence.

"Nope, he confirmed what the three chaps said – that she came down for a drink most days – and that she didn't like the name of the pub. She had an open tab at the bar too, so he wasn't best pleased about being two hundred quid down." He sighed and rubbed the back of his neck. "I'll go back and speak to the other neighbours, see if anyone knows anything else about her, and I've got the lads back at the station checking on next of kin."

Fi nodded along, but her eyes snagged on the local shop and the freezer just inside the door with a bright sign above it promising the best ice creams in the Cotswolds. How unprofessional would it be to get one?

"What's next on your list?"

"Hmmm?"

"You know, on the… magical side." The detective spat out the word 'magical' like it left a bad taste in his mouth.

"Oh, right, yeah. I've, uh, got some research to do. I thought I'd start this evening, after we've finished with the interviews."

Larry sniffed but didn't dissuade her. She took that as a good sign.

"How about an ice cream first?"

## Chapter 11

Fi hunched her shoulders as she sloped home. The interviews had been a complete waste of time. Lucille hadn't had any real friends. The nicest thing anyone had had to say about the old lady was that she was quiet after about nine o'clock and she kept her garden tidy. The only good thing was that the detective had agreed to an ice cream. She hadn't pegged him as a rocket lolly man, but then you never could tell. So, the only thing they had to go on was the weird state of her body. And magic was meant to be Fi's department.

She kicked a pebble off the pavement, scuffing her converse trainers.

"You OK?"

Fi looked up and into the cheery face of the magic club leader – what was her name? The lady was dressed in a sensible t-shirt and bright green cargo shorts. She hefted a canvas bag loaded with groceries onto her shoulder.

"Fine."

"It's awful about that lady, isn't it?" she said, falling into step with Fi. "I can't believe it all happened the same night as the club. It's made me wonder about how safe it is here and whether it's right to keep the club going, at least until they've caught the killer. Are you investigating? I mean the Magical Liaison Office, or is it the police? I've heard so many rumours about magic…"

"The police think everyone should go about their business. They're following up on several leads." A lie. One she had heard the detective trot off his tongue several times this afternoon. "And, yes, I'm involved."

"Oh good. That's really reassuring. I'd better go, get this milk in the fridge. Hope you catch them."

Fi grunted a thank you. Her phone buzzed. She took it out and collided with another pedestrian.

"Hey."

"Sorry."

"Fiona, right? From the other night. I heard about what they found on the field. Terrible stuff."

"Yeah," Fiona searched her memory for a name. "Frankie?"

"Finley." He corrected her. "What happened? I heard that old biddy was found. Awful. At least the kids will be able to play in peace now."

"You don't seem very upset." Fi tilted her head and regarded him.

He laughed nervously. "Well, I mean, you saw – she was a terror."

"Where were you last night?"

He giggled. "Wait, you're serious?" Fi continued to stare at him. He shuffled his feet and a sheen of sweat appeared on his lower lip. "Oh, well, I dropped the boys off, then went home, watched some tv with the missus, picked them up, put them to bed. Had a glass of wine, watched more tv then went to bed."

"What did you watch?"

"Celebrity ping pong. Have you seen it? It's great fun. I can't believe that they voted off Melinda, I would have gone for Cirian – the elf can sing, but he can't play ping pong for toffee."

"Right. OK."

"So, who do you really think did it?"

"I can't discuss an active investigation." That sounded official and maybe it would mean people would leave her alone to think. It sounded like everyone was pleased to see Lucille gone, only the blokes at the pub seemed to miss her.

He backed up a step. "Of course not. I'd better be off. Catch you later."

She turned back to her phone. A message from Maxi.

*Heard you got your first big case! Exciting, what! Good luck!*

Another message came in as she tapped a reply.

*Expecting your report. Keep me updated.*

Fi groaned. Agent Jones wanted a report. What was she going to say? There was a dead body. Magic probably involved. No leads. A third message popped up on her phone.

*Don't forget your training tomorrow.*

Fi groaned again. She had completely forgotten she had her first Magical Liaison Office training session tomorrow, and it didn't look like she'd get to skip it because she was in the middle of an active investigation. Fi swore and checked the details in her calendar. It wasn't even local.

She stomped home, frustrated with her own lack of knowledge about what to do next, annoyed that she had to write a stupid report and irritated that she had to go to a stupid training session instead of focusing on the case and she had no idea how she was going to get there.

Fi paused at the gate to her family home and her shoulders slumped. She'd have to ask for help. She called her sister.

"Hi Fi, how's it going? Found the killer?"

"No such luck and I've got to go to a training session tomorrow outside Oxford."

Fi could feel her sister's frown through the phone. "Oh, I'd have thought they'd have let you reschedule now you're in the middle of a case."

"Apparently not. Anyway, I was wondering…"

"Yes?"

"Can you give me a lift?"

"Oh. Normally I would, of course, but I'm working tomorrow."

"Right, right, and there's no way you can get to Oxford and back before you start?"

"Fi!"

"Sorry, sorry. But I can't take the bus, it'll never get there in time." Not with the three changes she'd need. It was as if Oxford was in another country. If she could drive, she could be there in an hour, as long as there wasn't any traffic. Maybe it was time to take some more lessons and upgrade her provisional license to a full one.

"And you can't get the train?"

"How am I going to get to Swindon? And then there's the change at Didcot." Oxford felt further away than ever.

"The surgery's closed tomorrow."

"So?" Had Agatha lost her mind? What did that have to do with anything?

"So…maybe Mort can give you a lift."

Fi's mouth fell open. Was her sister serious? That wasn't an option, even if she hadn't blown him off.

"Fi? Fi? Are you there?"

"Yeah, look, don't worry, I'll find my own way there."

Fi hung up. She felt her power crackle under her skin as her emotions swirled. She needed to blow off some steam. She flung open the gate and stomped over to her favourite corner of the garden, behind the Japanese maple trees, ducking through the hedge that blocked the compost pile from view. The leafy smell of decomposing soil filled her nostrils. She inhaled deeply and concentrated her power.

Electricity crackled to the surface of her skin and tickled along her body, raising her hairs and tingling through her skin. She channelled it into her palms and aimed at an old tree stump. She missed. Shaking out her hands, she aimed again. This time, the blue arc of electricity hit the tree directly on the large, singed knot off to the left.

She kept going until her power settled down. Then she walked over to inspect the smoking trunk. It was still intact, the veteran of too many of her outbursts to count in her teenage years. She sat on it and patted the familiar wood, worn smooth by years of her sitting on the top after her tantrums. She kicked her feet against the bark and stayed there for a few minutes, enjoying the peace of the garden, where no one expected anything of her.

When Fi stood, she still had no idea how she was going to move forward with the case or how she would get to Oxford tomorrow, but she did know that she craved company and snacks.

## Chapter 12

"Go! Go! Go!" Fi screamed into her headset. Her feet tapped under the desk, kicking against a discarded can of energy drink with a metallic chink. Cressida hissed at the sudden noise – she managed to infuse it with a note of disgust.

On the screen, her team surged forward, taking the building in a blaze of gunfire. She launched a grenade towards a likely hiding spot, her kill count rising as the explosion lit up the room.

"Ha! Great work!"

"High fives!"

The team celebrated with their traditional crazy dances, their on-screen avatars gyrating and circling.

"So, you want to go again?" Fi poured pretzels into her mouth and crunched them up.

"Sorry Fi-zar, got work tomorrow so I'd better call it a night."

"Come on Adrock, what happened to the guy who could game all night and still make it to work on time?"

"He hit middle age!"

"What about you Gilroy?"

"Sorry, the little lady's about to wake up so I'd better go."

"Still doing night feeds?"

"You know it. You're lucky you don't have any responsibilities, Fi."

Gilroy signed off.

"So, what's going on Fi?"

"What do you mean?"

"Come on. You stormed that last tower practically on your own and you want to start another round at midnight. You're spoiling for a fight, and not in a good way."

Adrock was right. Sometimes it galled Fi that her best friend was someone she'd never met in real life. He lived hours away, holed up in his flat in Scotland. It would be so much easier if she could find someone to connect with who didn't live over a hundred miles away. An image of the local doctor flashed through her mind and she shook her head to drive that distraction away. She wasn't relationship material, as her ex had told her a hundred times.

She sighed and logged out of their online game, but left her headset connected to the Discord channel they used while playing.

"I just…I'm in over my head at work and I'm back living at home. I thought I was OK with it, but I'm a failure."

"The Fi I know isn't a failure, she's our best sharpshooter!"

"Yeah, well life isn't as easy as a videogame."

"You want to talk about it?"

"Not unless you've got any ideas about magic rituals."

"In real life or in a game?"

"Real life. It's my job now." The group might not have met in person, but they were still close and shared life events through the lens of blowing stuff up on a screen. She'd happily shared her news when she'd first got the job; now she wasn't so sure she should have celebrated.

"Supernatural issues, huh? That sucks. Are you close to the protests?"

Fi frowned and typed 'supernatural protests' into her search engine. Sure enough, there were pictures of angry people holding cardboard signs with 'Supernaturals go home' painted in sloppy black letters. The Houses of Parliament loomed in the background. London.

"No, they haven't reached us yet."

"Well, you're always good at finding a different angle. Remember when we were all geared up to storm the castle and then you found that back entrance…you'll figure it out."

"Yeah, I guess."

"Shame there aren't any books about what you're after."

Fi started. She'd searched online – using incognito mode, there was no way that googling blood magic or ways to kill people and remove all their blood was going to look good in her search history – but she hadn't considered opening a book.

"Thanks Adrock, that's a great idea!"

"I do have them every now and then! Catch you next time."

Fi barely said goodbye before she logged out of her computer, yanked off her headset and ran out of the room. Cressida opened one bleary eye and huffed before following after the energy-drink driven witch.

Fi paused outside the library. It was always wise to treat the house with respect and the Bed & Breakfast was currently full of guests, so the last thing she wanted was to have the house slamming doors in her face. She tried the door handle. It opened. Good. The house wasn't playing games tonight.

She entered the room. A flash of gold darted through the door as Fi closed it.

"You didn't have to come."

*You're messing about in a sentient house's library. Someone has to watch out for you.*

"Thanks."

Cressida stretched out her small wings and jumped up onto the long, leather sofa.

*What are you looking for?*

"Not sure." Fi pulled a book at random from one of the built-in shelves that lined the room. *A Witch's Guide to Herbs.* That wasn't going to help. She reached for another. The gold lettering on the spine read; *Fae – how to recognise the fairy folk and avoid their traps.* She sighed and pushed it back in so hard that the thick cover thudded against the wall behind the shelves.

*How are you going to find anything in here? There's no order to these books.*

The house shuddered and Fi apologised before hissing at her familiar. "Be nice about the house, or it'll kick us out of here."

Fi stopped pacing around the room.

*Fine. Sorry. But how are you going to find what you want.*

"Mum normally just asks the house." Fi cleared her throat. "House, I'm looking for books about magic rituals. Please."

A shudder ran through the books with a rustling papery noise. Fi turned slowly. Nothing had moved. She frowned.

*Maybe you need to be more specific.*

Fi thought for a moment. "Any rituals involving blood magic."

This time there was a noise like a sharp intake of breath and the books began to shake.

"Oh no…"

Footsteps pounded down the stairs, coming closer. Fi winced and turned to face the door as Nell burst through, her chest heaving under navy, silk pyjamas.

"Why does the house think you're looking for blood magic rituals?!"

## Chapter 13

Fi explained everything to her mother, who had sunk onto the worn leather sofa and gripped her matching dressing gown in her slender hands at the mention of possible blood magic. The older witch had got up without a word and sought the comfort of a cup of strongly brewed tea and now they both sat in the library, staring at the shelves.

Fi sipped on her hot chocolate. She was wired enough thanks to three cans of caffeinated energy drink that coffee had seemed like a bad idea.

"You're sure?" Nell's voice was quiet, her skin ashen.

"I'm not sure about anything but it has to be dark magic, right?"

Her mother took another drink of her milky tea and placed the china cup delicately back on its saucer. She rolled up her sleeves and squared her shoulders.

"Well then, everything we have on blood magic, if you would be so kind."

There was a pause, then the house responded to Nell's request. A shimmer passed through the room and books moved from their places, sliding their spines along until they rested on the very edge of the shelves.

The two witches collected the dozen or so books and laid them on the low coffee table in the middle of the room. One of the covers had a tattoo on it. Fi shuddered. It looked like the rumours were true and there were books in here bound in human skin. She left that one alone and instead reached for a more normal looking book. Normal being a relative term in a library where books moved, and the typeface skittered across the page.

Two hours later and all Fi had learned was that she didn't want to be involved with blood magic. Ever. Most of the books she'd waded through contained page after page of dire warnings for magic users who reached for powers beyond their understanding. Some even had diagrams. Fi shuddered.

The artists seemed to revel in depicting ever more horrifying fates for those who dabbled in blood magic; wizards and witches sucked into dark portals from which barbed tentacles protruded; a wizard turned inside out – literally; a warlock driven mad and digging her eyes from her face with clawed fingernails. It was enough to turn anyone off dark magic. There were even detailed drawings of demonic runes with dire warnings never to invoke a creature from the dark realms and pictures of hollow-eyed cultists who gave their life force to their leader and the demon.

But nothing that mentioned how exactly blood magic worked or why a magic user would drain a body of its fluids.

Fi put down another book and rubbed her eyes. It was late. So late it was now early in the morning. Her mother stretched.

"Let's call it a night. I've got to be up in two hours to make breakfast for the guests."

Fi shook her head. "Let me just look at one more book." She grabbed the nearest volume; a thick book with a burgundy cover.

"I don't think you're going to find much in *A History of the Schism*. We all know that Mordred used blood magic, but knowing about those old battles won't do much good."

"You don't think..." Fi swallowed and forced out the rest of her thought, "...Mordred might be back?"

Nell paused partway through putting the teapot back on the tray. "You know who would know, don't you?"

"Who?"

"Your colleagues at the Magical Liaison Office."

Fi swore. She'd forgotten she had training today, and still no way to get to Oxford, and it was four a.m.

Nell patted her on the arm. "You'll do better after some sleep."

Fi trudged upstairs with Cressida at her heels. She collapsed onto her bed fully clothed and started snoring.

## Chapter 14

Fi awoke to the annoying bleep of her phone alarm. She groaned and sat up. Her head pounded with the fuzzy headache that came from staying up most of the night drinking energy drink. Ugh. She needed more caffeine to chase the throbbing away.

She stumbled into the shower, knocked over the body wash and got foam in her eye, before she staggered out and got dressed.

*Is that what you're wearing?*

Fi looked down at her ripped jeans and baggy t-shirt. "What?"

*You might at least make an effort.*

Maybe the wyrm had a point. Plus it was too hot for jeans. She changed into an oversized t-shirt dress and pulled on some leggings so she didn't have to shave her legs. With a yawn, she held open the door for the wyrm and made to follow through. The door slammed shut.

"Ouch!" She pulled at the handle. It didn't budge. "Come on, not today!" The door stayed shut. With an exaggerated sigh, Fi turned to look at her room. Empty cans littered the floor like strange spaceships drifting between planets made from dirty clothes. Chocolate wrappers filled the gaps and blotted out the remains of the carpet. Fi swore and put the rubbish in the bin before dumping her clothes into the wash basket. She tried the door again.

"Come on! That's all I've got time to do, I promise I'll dust and hoover when I get back. I'll even polish! Please. Just. Open. The. Door." She pulled on the door at each word in the last sentence and, miraculously, it opened on the last word, sending her pitching into the bed.

"Thank you," she called up to the ceiling. She righted herself and took a step towards the stairs before she noticed the head peering out of a door further down the hall. She smiled at the guest and apologised for the disturbance before scurrying to the kitchen.

Cressida was already munching on some burned toast and charred bacon in her spot near the aga, while Nell prepped for the breakfast rush. Her mother's hair was back in its neat chignon and only the faintest smudge under her eyes betrayed her lack of sleep. Fi tied her own hair back into a ponytail with a hairband she kept on her wrist and made a strong cup of Goblin Blend coffee. Black. With three sugars.

She plonked herself onto one of the wooden chairs around the large kitchen table and rubbed her eyes before she helped herself to a piece of toast.

"What time does your training start?"

"Eight o'clock."

Nell frowned at the wall clock. "And how are you getting there?"

"Bus, I guess."

"You'll never make it to Oxford by eight if you take the bus."

Fi shrugged. "Then I'll be late." She was so tired, would it really matter if she crawled back into bed for an hour or so?

"You can't be late for your first training session!" Nell turned from the range cooker and placed her hands on her hips. Fi cringed. She felt like a teenager again.

"OK, well what do you suggest?" Fi resorted to sarcasm. Definitely acting like a teenager.

"Fly." Nell dropped another piece of overcooked bacon onto Cressida's plate and turned back to the aga.

Fi gaped at her mother. "Fly? Just like that. It's over an hour to Oxford!"

"It'll be less if you fly. You've got a perfectly good broomstick; I don't know why you never use it."

Fi drank her coffee to stop herself from saying something she'd regret. See, she could act like a mature adult. She mulled over the idea. Flying would be faster than the bus. More reliable too. But not on a broomstick.

Fi finished her toast and checked the email on her work account. She entered the post code into the sat nav on her map app and walked over to her mum and Cressida. Fi bent down and stroked the small wyrm's head.

"Sorry, it says no familiars on the invite."

Cressida huffed.

"Not to worry, she can stay here with me. I need some company while I sort out who's going to run the bottle raffle. I can't have Harris trying to enter his homemade fire whisky again; we had three people in hospital last year!"

"Thanks Mum, and I'm borrowing the vacuum cleaner. Bye!"

Fi hurried to the cupboard under the stairs and grabbed the upright hoover. She went through the front door to avoid her mother and kicked off the tiled step, soaring into the air as her magic flowed into the vacuum cleaner.

Beneath her, Nell shouted up into the sky, "Bring it back in one piece!"

Fi smiled down and gave a jaunty wave as she headed further up above the rooftops. After a close call with a chimney, she wound the trailing power cable around the handle. She steered by leaning to one side and angling the machine so she could follow the main road. From her pocket, the electronic voice of her sat nav gave directions as if she were driving.

Fi rolled her shoulders back and enjoyed the breeze as the hoover speeded along. It was the first time she'd felt cold in two weeks thanks to the heat wave and already she could see hazy waves appear on the tarmac as the roads heated. She flew alongside a red kite testing the thermals before it wheeled away to find its breakfast with a screech.

As Fi flew past traffic jams caused by slow-moving tractors, she smiled. This was almost like the old times when she'd snuck the vacuum cleaner out to fly instead of using her broomstick. She'd always gotten on better with electrical goods...except when she blew them up, of course.

She shook her head and focused. A roundabout came into view. The dull roar of mounting traffic combined with the wind in her ears meant she couldn't hear the sat nav. Nothing for it. She descended and flew around the roundabout twice to get her bearings before zooming off along the main road heading for Oxford.

As distinctive spires and domes appeared on the horizon, Fi slowed down and pulled out her phone. Clutching it tightly, she checked the directions. The training centre was outside the city, thank goodness, so she didn't have to worry about no-fly zones or awkwardly riding the bus with a decade old vacuum.

Instead, she kept her phone out and followed the roads carefully, until she was hovering along over a dusty road between a row of trees. A red and white striped barrier zoomed past below her, matched by striped poles that stretched up into the sky. Fi zigged to one side to avoid them. Two uniformed guards shouted up from the ground.

"Halt!"

Fi craned her neck to better look at the guards and slammed into an invisible energy field. She screamed in pain as the vacuum cleaner pinned her arm against the hard barrier. Her neck whipped forward, and her head connected with the see-through shield. Dizzy, she lost control of her magic and the vacuum cleaner plummeted towards the ground.

## Chapter 15

She blinked as the road came into focus. With a yelp, she frantically pulled the hoover upwards. Just in time to avoid a headfirst collision with the ground, but not quick enough to save the vacuum cleaner. It scraped along the road with a sickening crunching sound, its dull moan turning to a screeching whine as it protested at the damage before it ground to a halt, smoke spiralling from the remains of the wreckage. The stench of burned electronics filled the air.

The two guards panted as they came to a stop by Fi. Both held crossbows. Aimed at her chest. Fi wobbled off of the hoover and fell to the floor.

"What do you think you're playing at? You can't fly onto government property without checking in!"

Fi blinked up at the speaker. He had two heads. Or was she concussed?

"Where's your ID?"

Fi fumbled in her pocket for her phone. It wasn't there. She panicked. Where was it? She got onto all fours. She had it in her hand...when she hit the ward. She looked around frantically, scanning the ground.

"ID. Now!"

"I...I dropped it. It's on the ground somewhere."

The first guard nodded at the second who holstered his crossbow and marched over to Fi, still scrabbling in the dust.

"Alright, miss. We'll take you back to the hut and talk. It looked like you banged yourself pretty hard on our protection ward, so we'll go, and Enson here will find your phone."

Fi groaned then cried out as he grabbed her injured arm. It looked like she didn't have a lot of choice. She staggered back to the hut, leaving the remains of the vacuum cleaner on the road for someone else to deal with. The vacuum cleaner - what was she going to tell her mother?

Inside the hut, the guard sat Fi on one of the wheeled chairs and got her a cup of tea from a battered tartan flask.

"Now, do you want to tell me why you decided to breach our barrier?"

Fi rubbed her head and winced. She could feel an egg-shaped lump raising up on her forehead. Another two guards thundered up to the small hut, crossbows out.

"I, uh, I'm meant to be in the training session."

The guard raised an eyebrow. "A likely story. All our trainees have to sign in." He grabbed a clipboard off the worn desk. He ran his finger down it. "Name?"

"Fiona Blair. Omensford Community Agent."

He frowned down at the paper. The other guard pushed his way in, waving her phone. He flipped open the leather phone case and found her provisional driving license. He held it out to the first guard, who grunted and passed it to Fi. She took the smashed smartphone with a sinking heart. Another phone dead. At least this one wasn't due to a power burst.

"Alright, this checks out. I'll get a healer sent over to fix you up. And next time, don't fly past clearly marked barriers."

The other guards relaxed and put away their standard issue crossbows.

"I've never seen a flying hoover before, made me think Henry had put something in my tea, it did."

"How did you get it to fly?"

"Er…" Fi was saved from their inquiries by an excitable fae with spiky green hair. She burst into the room like a firecracker and fixed on Fi with her bright green eyes. The fae strode forward and prodded Fi's forehead.

"Ouch!"

The fae nodded as if that confirmed something. "I'm Pinia, a healer. Want me to fix up your forehead?"

Fi nodded and tensed as Pinia held her long fingers over the bruise. Fi felt a brush of sweet magic, like cotton candy mixed with sherbet. It fizzed and the sharp pain in her head reduced to a dull ache.

"Are you injured anywhere else?"

Fi held up her arm. Pinia took it and moved it back and forward, ignoring Fi's grimace. "This will sting. How did you break your wrist?"

Fi gritted her teeth and focused on the fae's leather ear cuff as Pinia trickled her magic into the witch's arm.

"She flew into the protection ward."

Pinia squinted at the witch. "What did you do that for?"

"I didn't mean to!" Fi said through clenched teeth.

"And you're late. Gwen won't like that."

"Who's Gwen?"

"You'll see."

## Chapter 16

Fifteen minutes later, Fi was on the lawn outside an old manor house. Ivy crept up one half of the building, lending it a strange lopsided look at odds with the manicured lawn and trimmed trees. The grass was a bright green despite the heatwave. As soon as she was inside the protective barrier, Fi had felt the thrum of magic, no doubt preserving the centuries old building and gardens.

Fi was one of twelve recruits who stood in a neat semi-circle in front of a tall woman with grey, feathered wings sprouting from her back between the crossed straps of her tight sports top.

"You're late," said the woman. Fi opened her mouth to explain but the woman cut her off. "I don't want to hear it. Do better."

Fi shut her mouth and shuffled from side to side, determined not to do anything else that would upset the trainer.

"Right, now that we're all here," her storm grey eyes rested on Fi pointedly for a second before she turned her head, "my name is Gwen. I head up the field clean-up branch of the Magical Liaison Office, responsible for clearing up and containing any magical messes, but today, I am in charge of training you lot. This will be your first combat session and you will come to quarterly refresher training from now on.

"We don't expect our community agents to regularly engage in combat of any kind, but it never hurts to be prepared. Today, I will train you in the standard issue crossbows and basic self-defence. Who here has used any firearms or crossbows before?"

Two people raised their hands.

"OK, and does anyone have any magic or special abilities they'd like to share with the class?"

Fi raised her hand tentatively along with five others, unsure if there was a hint of sarcasm in the bird woman's tone.

"Right, well we'll see what you can do in a minute. First thing's first, you need to fill out your health and safety forms so you can't sue us."

A ripple of nervous laughter went around the recruits. Gwen didn't join in. The laughter died out. Fi pulled at her top as sweat prickled down her back. What had she let herself in for?

Someone raised their hand. "Do these forms tell us how to train safely?"

"Nope, but they protect the Office in case of serious injury or death."

The trainer handed out the forms and pens and Fi signed without reading it. She stared at Gwen's wings as the trainer spoke to one of the trainees who was pointing out some wording on the form about the use of lethal force. The feathers looked so soft and delicate, but somehow powerful at the same time.

"She's a harpy," said the bloke next to Fi.

Fi turned to look at him with a puzzled look on her face.

"Harpy; half bird, half woman. I'm Mosan." He held his hand out.

Fi shook it. "Fiona, but call me Fi."

Mosan nodded. "Hi Fi, you been to one of these before?"

"Nope. First time."

"Me too. Did you have to come far?"

"Omensford."

"Nice, we visited last year while we were on holiday. I'm based in Oxford."

"Easy for you to get here on time then," Fi joked, wishing she was more adept at social situations.

"Not with the traffic on the bypass! I only just got here on time."

"OK, now you're all happy with the forms, we'll start with a run," Gwen barked. She set off around the enormous mansion at a fast pace. Fi groaned and followed. She ended up towards the back of the pack. Maybe Cressida was right. She did need to exercise.

After three circuits around the old house, Gwen stopped and led them in stretches. Fi collapsed to her knees, panting. Her heart felt like it was about to explode out of her chest. She stretched out on the cool grass. She just needed to lie here for a minute and get her breath back…

"Now let's have some self-defence. Pair up!" Gwen barked.

Fi stifled a groan and forced herself back to her knees.

One trainee put up his hand. It was the same trainee who'd spoken up about lethal force earlier. "I have a black belt in Tae Kwon Do so I'd be happy to help you teach."

He didn't spot the glint in the harpy's eye as she smiled pleasantly and asked him to join her at the front of the class. She started a simple demonstration of how to break out of a wrist hold, but the trainee interrupted her. With a twist of her hips and a flick, he ended up on the floor gasping for breath. Fi winced on his behalf.

"Anyone else got anything they want to share?"

Everyone shook their heads. Behind her, blackbelt got up and launched himself at the harpy. Fi cried out a warning, but Gwen had already sidestepped and kicked him in a part of his anatomy that her mother would refer to as a 'gentleman's area'.

"In a fight, there are no points. Just a winner and a loser. Fight dirty. Fight anyway you can to stay alive and keep the other guy down. Any questions?"

The class shook their heads, more violently this time, keen to avoid being part of a demonstration. Gwen nodded. "Get on with it then."

Mosan gripped Fi's wrist, but she gaped at the student gasping on the floor until the harpy turned her eyes onto the tech witch and Fi redoubled her efforts to break out of Mosan's hold.

After two hours of bruising self-defence training, the harpy stopped them and had them line up at an archery range. She took a crossbow from a pile, aimed it with one hand and pressed the trigger. The bolt thudded into the centre of the target.

"The Magical Liaison Office uses crossbows as its weapon of choice. With the right ammunition, they are more suited to our purposes than guns and an operative can carry bolts for any situation; silver tips work against most supernaturals, our shafts are made from ash wood for fae and that doubles as a stake for any rogue vampires."

She hefted the crossbow onto her shoulder. "And of course, an arrow to the knee will slow anyone down."

Fi laughed at the videogame reference. No one else joined in and the harpy narrowed her eyes at the witch.

"OK, line up. Let's see what you can do."

She had them aim crossbows at archery targets set up under the shady trees until lunch. They started with standing targets before Gwen split a few trainees into a more advanced group and had them aim at moving targets. Fi wasn't selected.

Instead, she shot at the paper targets in shapes of all types of magical and mundane beings, reloaded and shot again, until her trigger finger was sore, and she was sure she could spot the difference in silhouette between a manticore and a chimera without thinking.

At lunch time, Gwen allowed them a half hour break.

"Any chance that healer could fix my bruises?" said Fi, only half joking.

Gwen glared at the witch. Fi backed away and joined the line for food. She held in a groan as she noticed it was only healthy food – soups and salad and not even a can of diet cola in sight. She sat down next to Mosan and a couple of other trainees.

"I don't agree with her teaching methods at all. I've got half a mind to put in a complaint!" the confident Tae Kwon Do blackbelt grumbled.

"I wouldn't if I were you," Mosan said. When the blackbelt narrowed his eyes and pursed his lips, Mosan continued, "Harpies hold grudges. If she finds out it was you, you'll be assigned to clean up gryphon crap lickety -split."

Fi looked up from her salad. "Is that true?"

He nodded and rearranged his glasses. "Heard it from the MLO agent who recruited me."

Tae Kwon Do looked as if he was about to argue but instead, he leaned back and lifted his chin. Fi stared back down at her plate, not wanting to get involved in any spats.

"Go on then, what have you had to deal with so far? I've had to move on a family of kobolds wild camping on the Dorset coastal path."

Fi felt herself instantly siding with the kobolds.

Mosan coughed. "I've mainly had to deal with complaints about noise from the university campus. They got hold of some illegal magical fireworks and nearly blew up the quad. But Oxford's a bit of a hotspot for magic."

"And you?"

Fi swallowed her mouthful of lettuce lathered with dressing. "There's some sort of blood magician on the loose back home…"

Everyone stopped talking and stared at her. She pushed the remains of her dinner around the plate as her face heated. She hated being centre of attention. She should have kept her mouth shut or told them about the pumpkin sightings.

Gwen strode into the room and clapped her hands together. "That's enough rest time. Back to work!"

# Chapter 17

For the afternoon session, Gwen split the magic users out from the group and another Magical Liaison Office agent led the humans in more self-defence and target practice. Gwen took the magic users round to the back of the house and behind a lichen covered stone wall that was so crooked, it looked like it might fall over in a strong wind. The lawn was less well kept here and wildflowers bloomed in colourful patches in the shade of the wall. Sturdy targets with concentric circles stood in a line.

"Alright, show me what you've got," Gwen ordered. Nobody moved. Gwen's eyes picked over the group and she selected someone at random. The hapless trainee walked up to the white line marked on the ground and raised his hands. A fireball erupted from his fingertips and flew towards the target. It hit to the left of the largest circle, leaving a singed mark on the white paint.

Gwen nodded. "Next!"

One by one the trainee agents demonstrated their power for the harpy. There was another fireball user who was so nervous under the harpy's stony gaze that she couldn't create anything larger than a candle flame, and a nature witch, who conjured a vine to attack the target. A werewolf admitted that she didn't have any magic, apart from her ability to transform into a large lupine predator. Gwen sent her to train with the humans. Finally, Fi was the only one left.

"Step up, Blair!"

Fi moved to the mark on the lawn. She tapped her fingers nervously on her thigh, unsure she could control her power. "I, uh, don't think this is a good idea."

"Just get on with it."

Fi shuffled her feet, feeling the hard ground through her thin-soled converse trainers.

"I need a baseline idea of what you can do before I give you any practice drills. I have to know what I'm working with, and you need to be able to control your magic in stressful situations or you'll be a danger to civilians."

That made sense. Fi called her power to the surface. It responded eagerly, happy to feel used instead of tamped down. She allowed it to flow across her skin, relishing the tingling sensation, feeling whole. Her arm hairs pricked up and her white hair stood up from her head in a static cloud. She raised her arms towards the target and pushed her magic into her hands. It glowed a hot blue and she released it.

The electrical bolt went straight through the target and hit the wall. Fi stared at the smoking hole where the target had been. Several stones crumbled out of the wall.

"Er, sorry."

The other trainees stared at Fi with wide eyes. Gwen strode over and patted her on the shoulder. The harpy pulled her hand away at the electric shock. Fi shoved her power back down.

"Sorry," she said again, looking down at her feet.

"No problem," Gwen said, sucking the heel of her hand. "That's what training is for. You have power, you need to learn to control it."

Fi looked up. The harpy didn't sound annoyed; she sounded impressed.

"OK, I want you spaced out and I'll give you some drills."

The trainees spread out. Fi noticed the gap between her and the purple-haired flame thrower was larger than the others. Gwen walked between the magic users and soon everyone was practicing either increasing their range or improving their aim.

Gwen approached Fi last. She walked straight past the witch and to a pile of replacement targets. She hefted the bulky round target easily onto one shoulder and set it up at the wall. A rogue fireball singed her wings, filling the air with the acrid smell of burned feathers.

"Easy Violet! Try to hit the target!" The purple-haired fire wizard hung her head and apologised. Gwen waved her off and turned her attention to Fi. "What I want you to focus on is control. I want you to hit the target, but not destroy it."

"Control. Got it." Fi drew her power to her hands again and loosed another bolt of electrical energy. The target disappeared. She swore.

The harpy kicked over the target and replaced it with another.

"You're in your head."

"What?" That didn't make any sense to Fi.

"You're overthinking it and you need to feel it. The magic is there, it wants to be used. Your body is a conduit. It's perfectly natural but if you force it or try to deny it, it will explode and that's when problems happen."

"Problems?"

"You wouldn't believe the number of messes I have to clean up because someone's bottled up their magic for years and then it explodes. Did you really think there were that many gas explosions in the UK?"

Now Fi thought about it, gas explosions were the perfect cover story for any type of magical disaster. It accounted for any damage and stopped the rising tensions between mundane and magical beings.

"So, what can I do to get more control?"

Gwen shrugged. "Breathe. Meditate. Feel the flow and stop being afraid of your power. It's part of you and that's not going to change."

With that, the harpy stalked off to supervise the other agents. Fi looked down at her hands. "OK, breathe."

She closed her eyes, took two deep breaths and allowed her electricity to swirl through her in time with the rhythm of her breathing. In and out. In and out. Her power felt good. It was just so destructive.

But it didn't have to be. The thought whispered through her mind like a caress. She paused, the electrical energy buzzing under her skin. She had brought Effie back from the dead thanks to her power...and she'd used it to fly a vacuum cleaner. Maybe if she wasn't so afraid of the damage she could cause, her power wouldn't spark out of control so often. She opened her eyes. No better place to try it out than in a special facility with healers on hand.

She let her electricity spark out of her slowly, a trickle at first, building to a small round ball in her hand. She aimed it at the target and instead of forcing it forward, she urged her power on more gently. Hit but don't destroy, she thought.

A moment later, there was a singed hole in the target. But it didn't go all the way through, and she hadn't destroyed it. She grinned and caught the harpy's eye. Gwen nodded. Fi tried again. And again. Was this what using magic was meant to feel like? It was so...right. She hadn't ever felt so positive about her power.

"Good. Looks like you're back in control." Gwen appeared behind her, making Fi's ball of electricity go wide. "Now, most magic users have some connection with their elements. They can sense them. See if you can do the same."

Fi stared.

The harpy sighed. "Close your eyes. Now, concentrate on your breathing. When you're ready, see if you can find any other electricity with your magic."

Fi did as she was told. She inhaled and exhaled, allowing her magic to fill her. She reached out. The harpy next to her crackled with electrical energy and a small ball of white sparks flamed in Gwen's pocket, her phone, perhaps. Fi's eyes shot open. "Wow."

"You felt it?" Gwen raised an eyebrow.

"That's incredible. It's like seeing the world in fireworks."

"Good. Keep on practicing. I heard you channelled lightning last year. I want you to try focusing on smaller amounts of electricity, see if you can sense it, then control it."

By the end of the afternoon, she was beaming, and a couple of the others had started talking to her again.

Gwen led them back to the front lawn at four p.m sharp. Mosan gave Fi a wave and walked over.

"How did it go?"

"Really good. You?"

"I'll be getting my black belt in no time," he laughed.

Gwen clapped her hands together and all the agents stopped talking and gathered round her like good trainees.

"Well done, you've completed your first combat training session…"

"Do we get our crossbows now?"

Gwen glared at the agent who dared to interrupt her. "You get the crossbows after you've passed the advanced training.

We don't just give them out." She paused until the student broke eye contact. "Now, you'll be back here again in three months, details will be sent to diaries. Class dismissed."

## Chapter 18

As the others dispersed, Fi stepped forward. "Er, can I talk to you for a second?"

Gwen raised one eyebrow, folded her arms across her chest and nodded.

"I need some help. I'm on a case but I don't know what to do next."

The harpy frowned.

"I mean, I think magic's involved but how do I find out more? I'm on my own and…"

"You're not on your own. You're part of the Magical Liaison Office; use them. Who's your superior?"

"Agent Jones."

"Jones?" the harpy laughed, her wings quivering. "Then you're in good hands. If she recruited you, she must have seen something in you. Remember: trust yourself, learn to control your magic and don't let it use you. Anything else?"

Fi shook her head. Gwen had confirmed her fears; Agent Jones expected her to do well and not bother her with stupid problems like not knowing what to do next.

"Alright, then get out of here." The harpy turned and strode back to the house. Fi watched her go before running after the other students.

"Mosan! Can I grab a lift? I need to replace my hoover!"

Mosan was kind enough to drop Fi at an industrial estate on the outskirts of Oxford where there was a large appliance store. Fi perused the vacuum cleaners on display. Her hand hovered over a standard upright – it would do the job and be a decent replacement for her mum, but a gleam of purple plastic caught her eye. She turned, hand still outstretched, to look at the modern, compact vacuum. It was advertised not as a household appliance, but as an 'experience' with an omnidirectional cleaning head, no dust bag, low noise and suction to rival a tornado. Fi read the large, printed sign promising a 'new era'.

An employee sidled up next to her, scenting a sale. His name badge read 'Tom – ask me about our price match promise'.

"Interested in the Suxor Platinum X-5000 are we? I don't blame you, it's state of the art cleaning technology. The best we've got in store. Here why don't you give her a whirl?" The salesman placed the cordless vacuum in Fi's hand with reverence and stood back.

With a flourish, he produced a Ziplock bag filled with brown dirt from his shirt pocket. He emptied the contents onto the floor and gestured to Fi. She bit her lip then stepped up to the mess, depressed the plastic trigger and the vacuum sucked up the soil with ease.

"It's got all the attachments for any of your cleaning needs; pet fur, long hair; deep pile carpets; hardwood floors; curtains. You name it, there's an attachment for it. And it's one hundred pounds off in our summer sale – personally I think someone in head office has messed up there – these things are flying off the shelves without any discount – but what do I know? I just sell the things – leave the details to corporate."

Fi smiled wryly to herself at his use of the phrase 'flying off the shelves'. Tom mistook her expression and smoothed his red tie down.

"I can see you need more persuading. The X-5000 has the longest battery life of any cordless hoover on the market today and, I'm not meant to do this, but, if you buy now, I'll throw in the spare battery too. No charge! You won't get a better deal this side of the A40."

"I don't know…it's a lot of money."

"Think of it like an investment, I mean, how often will you use it? Twice a week? If you add that up over a year, that's three pounds per use over ten years and I think that's a great buy. After all, you know what they say – buy cheap, buy twice! Anyway, I'll leave you to mull it over, but be quick; we close at five and I heard that we're repricing tomorrow…" Tom backed away and left Fi to think things over.

She looked between the two cleaners for a long minute, chewing her lip and tapping her toes. Was there something that happened when you turned thirty that suddenly made a person interested in appliance shopping? Five years ago, she would have grabbed the cheapest one and got out of the shop as fast as she could. But now...

She looked around to make sure the coast was clear then cautiously allowed a trickle of her magic to flow into the appliance. It purred and the battery symbol flashed up to one hundred percent charge. She bit her lip and focused her magic, sensing the electricity flowing through the appliance in a white wave of energy. With a thought, she cut it off. The vacuum stilled in her hand, and she smiled.

It would be a nicer vacuum cleaner for her mum to use in the B&B...and it would be more comfortable to sit on than the old hoover...and it wasn't like she was paying rent and she did have some money saved up. Fi had planned to save her earnings and move back into the small cottage that she had been forced to rent out when she'd lost her job in IT, but this would only put her back a couple of months, and it wasn't like she'd treated herself to anything else. She hadn't even bought a videogame in months. And she was a sucker for a gadget, especially an electronic one.

She made her choice, grabbed a large white box with a picture of the vacuum cleaner on the side and hefted it to the till. On the way, she paused at the mobile phone display and grabbed one. She pursed her lips and took another. She seemed to go through phones quicker than most people binged box sets.

"You went for it!" Fi smiled at the salesman's enthusiasm as he took her credit card. "You won't regret it. Now, can I do anything else for you?"

"Do you mind opening the box?"

The man's round face screwed up in puzzlement, but he clearly lived by the edict that the customer is always right because he dug under the counter for a Stanley knife and cut through the sturdy tape that held the box closed. Fi smiled and pulled the Suxor X-5000 out.

"They don't always have full charge straight out of the box, you know…" Tom started.

Fi smiled and allowed her power to flow into the new machine. The salesman's eyes boggled at the fully charged battery bar. Fi deftly assembled the X-5000 into its upright position before asking Tom to reseal the box and attach it to the vacuum with packing tape so she could get it home. Tom's face screwed up even further and his eyes darted around the store looking for help to deal with the crazy customer, but he did as she asked.

Once everything was secure, Fi carried the lightweight hoover, bulked out by the attached box, outside. The salesman leaned backwards to see what she was doing. His eyes widened further when Fi started the vacuum cleaner, and it hovered above the tarmac at hip height.

Fi tried to climb onto the X-5000, but the large box made it impossible for her to get comfortable sitting astride it. She settled for a side-saddle position and, satisfied, kicked off. The cordless vacuum responded to her power like it was made for her.

The last thing she saw as she zoomed up into the air was Tom's round face gaping up through the glass shop window.

## Chapter 19

Buoyed by her extravagant, but oh-so-worth-it, purchase, Fi enjoyed the flight home and got back in record time. The X-5000 might be her second favourite thing, after her gaming computer…oh, and her family. Obviously.

"What is that?" Nell stared at the purple and silver contraption strapped to a white cardboard box.

Cressida opened one emerald eye but stayed curled up in her spot near the range cooker, savouring the heat.

"Oh, I bought a new vacuum."

"Why?" Nell's eyes narrowed. "Did you blow up the old hoover?"

"No, actually," Fi said in a voice reminiscent of a teenager who's just got one up on their parent. Nell raised one eyebrow sceptically. "….I crashed it," Fi mumbled.

"Fi…"

"It's fine, Mum. I bought a new one, see I take responsibility for my mistakes, and this is a state-of-the-art vacuum. You'll love it. Just let me set it up…" Fi tugged at the packing tape. It didn't move, having, in the way of such sticking tapes, somehow got stickier and more tightly pressed during the journey so now it was practically indestructible. She gave up and retrieved the scissors from the kitchen drawer. With a few snips, she detached the box and demonstrated the new vacuum cleaner to her mum.

Cressida started at the low hum and hissed with the inbuilt distrust that all pets have for vacuum cleaners. She didn't move from her spot though.

Nell looked unimpressed. "I still don't understand why I need the power of a tornado to clean the floor… but thank you for replacing the one that you broke."

Fi smiled and packed the cleaner away with a friendly pat. She returned to the kitchen, poured herself a cup of coffee and opened the fridge to find something to eat. The lunchtime salad seemed a long time ago.

"Well, seeing as you're so responsible nowadays, you won't mind coming with me to the common tomorrow." Nell interrupted Fi's search for food. "Alf's arriving with the donkeys and I want to welcome him. It would be nice if we could bring him a gift…"

Fi sighed, knowing exactly what her mum was hinting at. "Fine, I'll make some scones. After I've had some food."

Nell smiled and nudged her daughter aside to pull out bread, ham and salad to make a sandwich. Fi leaned against the side, watching.

"I don't suppose you found anything else out about blood magic when I was gone?"

"I left some books out for you, but I don't think there's anything of use. Not that I could see, anyway." Nell handed her the sandwich and pursed her lips. "It's a bad business. I can't believe it's happened in my village."

"Hmmm," Fi said through a large bite. Her mum was taking this evil magic user personally. Not surprising given she ran the Witches', Wizards' and Warlocks' Institute and was practically an institution herself in the small Cotswold village. Fi opened her mouth to ask a question, but closed it again at Nell's glare. Talking with your mouth full was a sin in the Blair household. Fi swallowed.

"But it has to be a magic user, right? What about–"

"Before you say something you'll regret, I'm confident that none of the WWWI are using blood magic. You can't hide that sort of taint in magic, and no one's missed a meeting, except the werewolves…"

Fi raised her eyebrows at that. "You can't think Steve and Glen had something to do with it?! They've been on holiday at Centre Parks, they only got back last week."

"I'm not saying anything. I'm telling you who wasn't at our last meeting. Most likely you need to focus on someone who's not from round here, but you're the Magical Liaison Office agent."

"Community agent," Fi muttered under her breath as Nell swept out of the room, no doubt to study plans for the Donkey Derby.

*Feeling sorry for yourself, are you?* Cressida's voice rang in Fi's head.

Fi jumped. She was getting used to the psychic link with her familiar, but it was still unnerving hearing someone inside her head if she wasn't expecting it.

"Just stating facts. And the fact is, that I've got no idea who killed Lucille." Fi groaned. "And I've got to write up a report for Agent Jones."

*Maybe Agent Jones will be able to help.*

"Or maybe she'll realise she made a big mistake hiring me when she sees I've got no clue what I'm doing."

*True.*

Fi glared at the small wyrm. "You're not helping!"

If it was possible for a lizard to shrug, Fi would have sworn that Cressida shrugged before lowering her head back to the floor and closing her eyes.

Fi munched on the rest of the sandwich angrily. She tried practicing her magic, but it kept darting away, out of reach, reminding her she wasn't in control. Fi finished her sandwich and stood. She was going to read the heck out of those books and come up with a breakthrough in the case. Just as soon as she'd baked the scones. She slammed open cupboards and deliberately clanked ceramic bowls together while she got everything together.

Cressida opened her eyes again at the noise and hissed before stalking out of the door and into the garden. Fi huffed as she watched the small wyrm jump into the air to catch the small insects that flew low to the ground in the cooling evening air. Stupid wyrm. What did she know about anything? Weren't familiars meant to help their witches? All Cressida did was gripe and moan.

Fi mixed the ingredients by hand – after blowing the fuse in too many electric mixers, she'd learned it was easier that way. Plus, it meant she could take out the stresses of the day on the batter.

As her hands went through the familiar motions, Fi's mind worked in the background. She went over what she knew about the case; the position of the body, the strange method of death. Nothing new jumped to mind. So the method was weird and probably involved magic. She'd read the books her mum had left for her, that might fill in some gaps.

What about motive? So far, no one had liked Lucille, apart from possibly her drinking buddies down the pub. But would anyone kill her? Her next-door neighbour had seemed frazzled and annoyed but was that enough to make her a murderer? And the mum next door seemed an unlikely dark magic user.

She was missing something. That was the only thing clear about this case. With a sigh of frustration, she rolled out the dough and violently pressed it into circles before slamming the baking tray into the oven. As they baked, she poured herself another coffee. Tonight was going to be a long night of reading.

## Chapter 20

Fi turned her face into the breeze, it was refreshing and promised a hint of rain in the air. Wispy clouds twisted past in the blue sky. The heatwave would break soon, but for now, the ground was still baked hard, the grass was the same straw yellow, and the sun blazed above the large common. Nell strode across with confidence while Fi followed, carrying an old biscuit tin stuffed with home-baked scones, their sweet bread-like smell wafting through the gap where the lid didn't quite match up with the base.

Fi wondered how her mother could stand to wear tights in the middle of summer. The tech witch sported cargo shorts that hung below her knees, showing her pale shins. She had long ago given up on getting a tan, and her white legs reflected the sun's rays with a sheen of protective sun cream. Despite her vest top, beads of sweat gathered under her arms.

Beside her, Cressida sauntered, her head turned towards the sun as she enjoyed the heat. Nell looked cool as she walked past the barriers that made up the donkey's temporary enclosure. She headed straight for the colourful caravan that housed Alf and knocked smartly on the forest green door. While they waited for it to open, Fi followed the trailing floral pattern with her eyes; it was a symmetrical stencil in white, black and red that followed the curves of the caravan in colours made bolder by the summer sun.

The net curtains over the small window twitched and then Alf was at the door. He was a wiry man with hairy, muscular forearms that strained against his checked shirt, worn over a black vest. He grinned down at the two witches, rolling a long strand of dry grass between his teeth. Alf removed the grass from his mouth and descended the white steps with his arms open.

"Nell Blair, ain't you a sight for sore eyes. Let me look at ye." The short man enveloped Nell in a bear hug. She giggled and returned the hug. Fi rolled her eyes. Was her mother actually flirting? She shuddered.

"How did the winter treat you, Alf?"

The donkey wrangler released Nell and took a step back. He shook his head, his salt and pepper hair waving with the motion. "Not too bad, not too bad. We lost Wonky jus' afore Christmas, and I had to leave Hotay at the sanctuary, but the rest are raring to go."

"And your family?"

"Young Alfie's here with me this year, but you know how it is. The youngsters don't want nowt to do with the family business for the most part. The twins are off having a gap year before university – a gap year! When I was a lad, we had half a day on Sunday and that was the only time off. My old man worked every day of his life, so he did. A gap year, I ask you." Alf shook his head again at the folly of youth.

"I know, sometimes I think I don't know my own children," Nell said with a small sigh. Fi frowned behind her back.

Alf looked up and noticed the younger witch for the first time. "And young Fiona! Fancy a donkey ride?"

"Er, no thanks. I think I'm a bit big now." Fi glanced over her shoulder at the donkeys grazing in the field. They looked mild, nibbling away at the dried grass, but Fi remembered the vicious glint in the eye of the ass who had thrown her onto her arse partway through a race. Nope, donkeys were bad news.

"We-ell mayhap ye are, but these are sturdy stock, ready for the races." He leaned forward and put a hand next to his face conspiratorially. "If I was you, I'd put my money on Burrito over there, you see? The one with the tan patch, he's a crafty one and no mistake."

*Hah! That bag of bones! I'd wager he gets confused and goes backwards,* Cressida said before she slunk over to the pen to assess the donkeys.

"Thanks for the tip." Fi smiled and held out her biscuit tin.

Alf took it and cracked the lid, breathing in the aroma of freshly baked scones. "Hmmm, always a pleasure to come to Omensford for your cooking Nell."

The older witch giggled again. "Oh Alf. These are my daughter's recipe."

"That so? Well, she must have learned to cook from the best." He grinned at Nell, showing his yellow teeth and put the blade of grass back between his chapped lips. "So, what's the set up this year?"

Fi wandered over to join Cressida as Nell talked through the racecourse positioning, the placement of each stall and where Alf could get water for his steeds.

"…And, of course, there's the new age limit this year for riders."

Alf shook his head again. "I don't know what the world's coming to Nelly, back in my day, you sat a child on a donkey and that was that. Now it's all health and safety and 'don't let them ride without a helmet'."

"Parents will sign a waiver, naturally, but you have to admit we don't want a repeat of last year's incident."

Alf winced at the reminder. Fi remembered that crash; it had been the front page on the local paper for three days. *Donkey Disaster! Asses Collide in Derby Danger Race!* Three children had been hospitalised and the WWWI had put in place strict rules for future derbies, including; riders must wear helmets at all times, a minimum age of nine years old for riders and the signed health and safety waiver from parents or guardians.

And not before time, in Fi's view. Her own donkey riding career had ended with a bruised coccyx at the tender age of six and she hadn't trusted a donkey since. She wandered closer to the creatures and watched as they grazed, brown eyes blinking innocently, tails flicking at the flies that accompanied all donkeys.

"Hello!" Agatha's voice carried across the common.

"Little Aggy! As lovely as your mother." Alf smiled. "And Bea, you ready to ride this year?"

"Can I? Please?"

"How old are you, lass?"

"Seven and a half."

"Sorry, you can't be in the race…"

"Aww, that's not fair." She reached out and patted the soft fur of the closest donkey.

"…But I can give you a ride tomorrow."

A couple of local kids that Fi recognised from the magic club arrived to look at the donkeys. "Can we have a ride?"

Alf shook his head. "They've had a long couple of days travelling, but they'll be ready to go for the derby."

Agatha sidled up to Fi. "Nice ass."

Fi smiled. She couldn't help herself. "Don't be a smart ass."

"Bit ass-inine, aren't you?"

"Big ass-umption."

Agatha bit her lip as she thought, then; "Stop being p-ass-ive aggressive."

"Really?"

Agatha shrugged.

"You should be embarr-ass-ed by that!"

Agatha nudged Fi with her shoulder and groaned. Fi grinned. She had won this round of silly puns, the game that always made her feel closer to her sister.

*You're both asses!*

"That's not how the game works, Cress."

*Cressida!* The small wyrm hissed.

"Well, we'd better be off. I've got stalls to supervise." Nell waved and left the donkey owner to deal with the growing crowd of children looking for entertainment in the sleepy town.

"You know where I am, stop by any time," Alf replied as he returned the wave.

Fi screwed up her face at Nell's back.

"And you can stop pulling faces, young lady." Fi gaped. Sometimes she could swear that her mother could read minds. "Now, make yourself useful and help Steve with the tent pegs."

Her phone rang before she could think of an excuse to get out of helping. She answered it without checking the caller ID. Detective Ledd's gruff voice sounded down the line.

"There's been another murder."

## Chapter 21

Fi raced across town to the location that the detective texted her. Fi slowed, panting, as she approached the familiar school building. Unlike most of the town, it was built from red brick; a large Victorian construction with a sturdy, symmetrical frontage topped by triangular points. Fi swallowed and her gaze raked over the line of the building. Some buildings have the power to transport you back through time and Fi had a lot of memories of the school; few of them good.

The pants-wetting apprehension of the first day rolled over her like a wave, followed by the cruel laughter of children when her hair had stood on end as her power mounted. Fear came next. She hadn't meant to shock Clarissa, her one-time best friend, but it had inevitably happened. After that, no one had really spoken to her much, except for her sister and Agatha's friend, Liv.

She swallowed the unwelcome feelings and the surge of power that came with them. Draped around her shoulders like a scarf, the small wyrm purred at the electricity brushing against her scales. The detective stood outside the iron gates, waiting for her. She forced her shoulders down and walked over. He offered her his hand, and she took it.

"Ouch!" Detective Ledd withdrew his hand at the shock, shaking it. "That was some static."

Fi smiled nervously and rubbed her own hand on her shorts. She hadn't tamped down her power enough.

The detective squinted at her, his eyes almost disappearing in his piggy face. "You ready to see the body?"

Fi nodded. "Lead the way."

He gave a grunt of acknowledgement and Fi prepared herself. They walked through the school, past the computer lab. The one place where Fi had actually felt at home, until she'd destroyed all the computers thanks to one of her power surges. It had taken months of fundraising to replace the equipment. Lonely months of standing to one side in the playground at lunches instead of playing online games under the disinterested eye of one of the teachers.

The detective didn't notice her inner turmoil and carried on through the large hall, lined with wooden bars for the times when it doubled as a gymnasium. Fi looked up at the ceiling. Yep, the climbing ropes still coiled neatly, waiting to be pulled down for the torturous game that PE teachers liked to play; let's laugh at the weak kids who can't climb a rope.

Fi followed the detective through another door and they were in the sports field. Fi hurried after him, hugging herself as memories of wet days when they were forced to play hockey rang through her mind. Not that she actually played hockey. She mostly sat on the bench, rain trickling down the back of her PE kit and, when she was made to get onto the pitch, she hung back, well away from any ball or opposing player.

She almost walked into the detective, who had stopped by the sports hut. The plain, corrugated iron building was a testament to practicality over aesthetics and contained all the school's torture items, Fi shook her head, no; sports equipment. And there, in front of the open door, was the body.

Fi was prepared this time, and it was only later that she wondered if there was something wrong with her that she could be prepared to see a corpse. A dry, shrivelled body dressed in men's clothes lay curled on the ground next to a netted bag full of footballs.

"Cause of death?" she asked as Cressida climbed down her body and circled the corpse.

"Tell your dragon to stay away from the evidence!"

*I'm a wyrm! Although, I can see how small minds might not appreciate the difference between our species. Dragons are only the size of a bus, after all. It's an easy mistake to make. And I'm not messing with any evidence, I'm helping...unless he possesses a superior sense of smell?*

"She says she's being careful."

Cressida huffed and the detective continued to eye her as she prowled around, sniffing the dry ground.

"Coroner will need to confirm it, but the throat's been cut again."

"Who is it?"

"His ID badge says it's one of the teachers, but we'll have to confirm that at the autopsy as his face doesn't exactly match the picture." Detective Ledd handed Fi the ID. It showed a plain man with dark hair. In the way of all ID photos, it didn't show him at his best, unless his best was a vacant stare and the awkward grimace that people do the instant a camera is pointed at them, but there was some resemblance to the dried husk on the floor. The neat, printed lettering said that his name was Sam Hackett. Fi's brows furrowed. She knew that name.

"He died a couple of hours ago, as best we can tell. He ran a football club on Saturday mornings. We've called up a few parents and they said the club went ahead as normal. He must have been putting the balls away when he was killed."

*Brimstone.*

"Again?"

The golden wyrm nodded and then sniffed away in another direction.

Fi walked around the deceased teacher, careful not to touch him. "Cressida says there's more brimstone here…How tall do you think he is…was?"

Detective Ledd frowned. "About six foot I'd guess. Why?"

"How easy do you think it is to cut someone's throat from behind? You'd have to be tall, right? If your victim was six foot. And why would you turn your back on someone holding a knife?"

"He could have been slashed from the front."

"He wouldn't just stand there, though. He's a PE teacher – an athlete. Why wouldn't he run?"

"Unless they didn't know the killer had a knife. It's not like murderers advertise that they're going to kill their victims. Not in real life anyway," the detective countered.

Fi drummed her fingers against her thigh. "Or maybe, they trusted the killer enough to turn their back on them…"

Detective Ledd didn't even bother to get out his notebook and jot Fi's theory down.

*Over here.*

Fi's head snapped round to a bench on the other side of the field. She hurried over. Cressida sat next to a thermos flask, her tail curled neatly around her clawed feet.

*This smells of him.*

"That could have been left here weeks ago."

*It's too fresh.*

She called the detective over and pointed out the flask. He screwed up his face but bagged up the tartan thermos into an evidence bag, the contents sloshing inside.

"Do you want to come to the autopsy? This is getting towards serial killer territory so Robbie's doing it ASAP."

Fi huffed out a breath, but she nodded. Attending autopsies looked like it was part of the job. Plus, it meant she'd be too busy to write up the report.

## Chapter 22

The autopsy was much the same as the first one. Fi thought she was prepared, but the overwhelming scent of antiseptic, flowers and the underlying sickly-sweet smell of decay still made her gag. Robbie was almost apologetic that she couldn't tell them anything new, but she agreed to test the tea. Although, what she was testing for, none of them could say. It wasn't like there was a test for blood magic or brimstone.

Or was there? Something else for Fi to look up when she got home. She made a note on her phone as she got into the detective's cramped car. Cressida curled up on her lap, an unwelcome hot water bottle in the small, stuffy car.

"What's next?" she asked.

Larry grunted as he manoeuvred out of the drive and back onto the road. "Interview his neighbours, some of the parents and kids from the school. See if anyone knows anything." He didn't sound hopeful. Suddenly, he hit the steering wheel with the palm of his hand. "Bloody magic! It's always bloody magic round here." He shot a sideways glare at Fi. "I didn't sign up for this. I didn't want to deal with bloody cults and what have you."

Fi twisted up her face, trying to understand the detective's outburst.

"And what do the bloody Magical Liaison Office give me to help?" Fi opened her mouth then shut it again as he carried on. "Some wet behind the ears recruit who doesn't know the first thing about magic." He shook his head and slowed down to let a tractor pull onto the road.

*Are you going to let him talk to you like that?*

"I am a witch, you know." Gah, she sounded like her mother.

"What?"

"I do know about magic. I'm a witch."

Larry blinked at her. "Well, what's going on then? We're one body short of a serial killer and nobody's happy. It's a miracle it hasn't made it into the press yet."

*You shouldn't let yourself be bullied by that mundane idiot.* Cressida hissed menacingly and Fi stroked her head to calm the small wyrm.

Fi swallowed. "I'm looking into leads. Same as you."

He grunted again. "I had someone at the station look into all the newcomers to the area in the past six months–"

"Why?"

Larry squinted at Fi, like she was stupid. "The murders happened recently, right. Stands to reason it's not someone who's lived here for years. Why would they start killing now?"

Why, indeed? thought Fi as the detective continued.

"Anyway, there's only one couple who's moved in, down on Hill Street, so, I thought we'd talk to them too."

Fi's heart sank. She had a bad feeling about where this was going. "What's the address?" she asked innocently.

He retrieved his notebook from his pocket and handed it to her. "Last page. Do you know it?"

She flicked through and suppressed a groan. "I own it."

## Chapter 23

Fi stared at the address scrawled in the leather-bound notebook. It was her old house. The house she currently rented to a lovely young couple, who were almost too well behaved as tenants.

Detective Ledd swerved the car. Errant blackberry brambles scraped along the paintwork. He got the steering wheel back under control just in time to avoid careening into the ditch that lined the side of the road. To his credit, the detective didn't swear. But he looked like he wanted to.

"What do you mean it's your house?"

"I mean, I own it. I rent it out."

"I thought it sounded familiar…" The detective trailed off. Fi tapped her fingers against her thigh as her thoughts drifted back to the first time she had encountered the detective, when he had knocked on her door to investigate her for the murder of a local woman.

"And you did background checks on these people." Larry's voice cut through her thoughts.

Fi bit her lip.

"Right?"

"I checked they could afford the rent, and I did an online check. Nothing suspicious." That was true. She had searched for them on the internet and found the usual social media pages. She had even befriended them online and was treated regularly to pictures on her feed of the two of them having barbeques in her garden.

"OK then. Well, they live next door to some werewolves, so we can talk to them, too."

Fi frowned. "Why do we need to talk to Glen and Steve?"

"Well," the detective coughed, "you know…" He gestured with his hands. "Werewolves. Natural killers."

Cressida hissed her displeasure at his statement.

"Glen and Steve wouldn't kill anyone! And even if they did, they wouldn't leave the bodies like that." Fi stopped, aware that she wasn't helping her case. "I mean, werewolves don't use magic like witches and wizards. They couldn't drain the blood like that. And Robbie would have mentioned teeth marks."

"Hmmfph."

The rest of the car journey continued in uncomfortable silence. Fi fumed at the detective's not so concealed prejudices and when they reached her old house, she slammed the car door shut to vent her frustration. She considered overloading the sparkplugs…she didn't do it, but it was a close call.

For his part, the detective stormed up the neat garden path to the front door and hammered on it with his fist. No one answered.

Fi got out her phone. She found what she was after and waved it in the detective's face.

"They're away on holiday. Look." She scrolled through pictures of cerulean seas and sandy beaches. "They've been away since last week, which means they couldn't have killed Lucille or Hackett." She tried to keep the triumph out of her voice.

"That could all be faked. You're the landlord; let us in."

"Isn't that an invasion of privacy?"

"Just do it. If there's nothing there, all good. If there is something, we can stop a killer."

Fi rolled her eyes. "I'll do it. To show you you're wrong."

She dug out her keys and let them in. Once inside, she let the detective poke around while she took a meter reading; might as well give herself a decent excuse to be in the property. She caught up with the detective in the kitchen.

*They've got better taste than you.* Cressida nodded towards a glass vase framed in one of the paned windows.

The wyrm was right. It looked like it belonged there.

"Don't break anything." Fi scowled at her familiar. The wyrm had a penchant for destroying ceramics and glassware that she didn't like, which meant that most of Fi's mugs had been destroyed. Fi picked up a picture of the happy, smiling couple in a sky-blue frame, annoyed that they looked like they had their lives together. Her thoughts wandered to a certain doctor…maybe they could take cheesy pictures together like that…if she hadn't been such an idiot and ruined any chance they had of having a relationship. She shook her head and put the frame down.

"Found anything?"

Detective Ledd shook his head as if he was disappointed not to have found a murder weapon or occult sigils scratched into the walls.

"Can we go then? I'm not sure how legal it is for me to be in here without giving them notice."

Fi led the way outside and locked up.

"Hi there! Everything alright?"

Steve waved from over the fence. He had three different neon bags slung over his broad shoulders. His daughter, Zadie, pirouetted on the patch of lawn as Glen locked the door.

"Fine, I…had to take a meter reading."

The werewolf eyed the detective, who met his gaze with a defiant chin tilt.

"Not investigating anything then?"

"Er…"

"As it happens, Mr Loupin, we are investigating a murder. Where were you this morning?"

"This morning?" Steve replied while Glen let out a low growl under his breath at the detective's question. "Well…we took Zadie to football practice like usual…"

Detective Ledd arched one bushy eyebrow at Fi. It reminded her of a fuzzy caterpillar inching across the ground. She could read the thoughts on his flabby face; football practice. With the PE teacher.

"...then some of us parents went out for brunch with the kids afterwards. We only got in about an hour ago and now we're off out again for swimming, then recorder lessons and I've got to squeeze in a shop. Come on Zadie, let's go."

"Is this about the old lady on the common?" Glen asked.

"What do you know about it?" The detective had his notebook out in an instant.

Glen's eyes flashed. "Only what I heard at school pick up."

"You weren't at the common this week then? No urges to run under the moon?"

"No."

"Alright, thanks, both." Fi butted in before Glen decided to make a complaint. There was no way that Steve or Glen would have had the time to kill anyone and go for brunch.

"Before you go, did you know Sam Hackett at all?"

"Zadie's football coach?" Steve scratched his chin, dislodging one of the bags which fell to the ground with a thump. "Not really, he kept himself to himself. Bit grumpy if you ask me. We were thinking about taking Zadie out of the class after he threw a dodgeball at Kyle, but she does love her activities, don't you dear?"

Zadie looked up from a flower she had been studying. "Fairies don't like it if you pull their wings off."

Fi repressed a shudder. Zadie creeped her out.

*Is that child all there?* Cressida echoed her thoughts with eerie precision.

Fi clamped her mouth shut.

"That's right, dear. Now we've really got to get going or we'll be late for swimming." Steve pushed his way out of the neat garden gate, shepherding his daughter in front of him. As the gate swung shut, he turned back. "You might want to try down the pub. I think he drank there a bit."

"But he was a PE teacher."

Steve shrugged. "I guess they still drink. Gotta go. Bye!"

"Good day," Glen said as he followed them out of the gate, his tone chilling the warm air.

Detective Ledd and Fi watched Steve manhandle the bags and Zadie into his sensible sedan car while Glen got in the driver's seat, and Fi gave them a wave as they headed downhill to the pool.

She resisted the urge to say 'I told you so' to the detective and instead opened the gate and followed him onto the pavement.

"Pub?" she asked.

## Chapter 24

Outside the Witch's Brew, Jack and Jeremy sat, their tans contrasting darkly with their stained white vests. They sweated under bucket hats in the persistent heat.

"Afternoon Officers." They raised their nearly empty pint glasses as one.

"This heat has got me properly quanked," one of them said, leaning back as he finished his drink.

"Aye, it'll sap all your strength."

"Alright boys, don't suppose you know a Sam Hackett?" Detective Ledd ignored the conversation about the heat wave and sank down onto a picnic table and leant forward with a false joviality.

"Aye, he was here from time to time."

"Not much of a talker mind ye. I think he was a teacher."

"A fitness teacher," Fi supplied.

Jack, or maybe Jeremy, nodded sagely. "That'd be about right. I asked him to join our tug o' war team, but he wouldn't go for it."

The other old man shook his head in sympathy. "We could've won against St Columba's if he'd have joined us."

"He never drank with you then?"

Jeremy and Jack shook their heads together, reminding Fi of the bobble heads that sat on car dashboards.

"Thank you, gentlemen." The detective stood and went inside.

"'Ere, 'as summat 'appened to 'im?"

Fi paused mid-step and turned back. "He's dead."

The two men raised their eyebrows, gave a grunt of acknowledgement at the passing of someone they didn't know well, and each took a swig of his drink. Fi left them to it and entered the pub. Her eyes adjusted quickly to the gloom. She nodded to the magic club leader sat in a corner with a fizzy drink, and walked over to where the detective chatted to the barman. In the way of all bartenders, Brian rubbed the inside of a pint glass with a faded green towel that had the name of some brand of beer emblazoned on it.

"…yeah, he came in here a bit. Normally after a weight-training session, or so he said. He liked to say that he'd earned his pint…guess he won't be paying his tab either." The bartender sighed and paused his cleaning for a moment to mourn the loss of his cash.

Detective Ledd scribbled on his notepad. "How much was on his tab?"

"About fifty quid."

Fi pressed her lips together to stop herself commenting that the Witch's Brew needed to change its policy on tabs. This interview wasn't getting them anywhere. Bored, she decided to try sensing electricity while the detective asked more questions. She shut her eyes and placed her hands on the wooden bar. Fi reached out with her magic and sparks flared in her mind. The bartender and detective lit up with faint electrical signatures, but above her and all around the pub, the cables that carried electricity to the appliances flared. She swayed and opened her eyes, blinking away the white map from the inside of her eyes. The lights flickered and Detective Ledd gave her a warning look.

Brian eyed the bulbs. The detective leaned forward, resting his elbows on the bar. "Did he ever get into any trouble?"

Brian put down the pint glass and picked up another. "He didn't get into any fights round here if that's what you mean. He kept himself to himself really, except if there were any families in, he'd sit in the corner staring at them and he'd finish up his pint right quick and leave."

"What do you mean he'd stare at them?" Fi asked.

The bartender shrugged. "Just that. I don't think he liked kids...or magic for that matter. He talked to me a couple of times about changing the name of the pub, but some people are like that. I mean, I wouldn't get half as many tourists if it was called the King's Arms or something, would I?"

Larry thanked him for his time, and they headed out.

"Time to check out his house."

## Chapter 25

Much like Lucille, Sam Hackett had lived alone. Fi stared at his flat. In a town full of sandy coloured houses made from local Cotswold stone, the brick building stood out. It spoke of the council's poor town planning decisions several decades ago, although luckily the council at the time had had the foresight to relegate the small block of flats to the other end of the village, well away from the picturesque town centre.

Detective Ledd had a key, retrieved from Hackett's body, and he let them into the building. Hackett lived on the ground floor, to the right of the entryway. Larry unlocked the door to the flat.

The apartment had the peculiar smell of 'man living alone' that made Fi instantly want to open a window. Instead, she held her arm over her nose and picked her way past stacks of magazines, following the detective.

Cressida took one whiff and choked. *It's worse than your bedroom after one of your all night sessions.*

She informed the witch that she would wait outside, where she curled up on the pavement next to the entrance.

The walls were a pale off-white that looked like it hadn't been updated in at least a decade, with a couple of pictures hung from nails that jutted from the walls. Fi tried not to look at the exposed flesh on display, but seriously, in order to do that pose, the woman would have to have had her spine removed.

A pentagram caught her eyes in the stack of magazines. She pushed aside the nudey magazine on top, resisting the urge to wipe her fingers on her dress. It was some sort of anti-magic propaganda called the 'True Race'. Fi's eyes roamed over articles titled 'How mages killed off humans' and 'Ten best weapons to use against vampires' and 'how to spot demons' – that article had swirling symbols dotted across the page that made Fi shudder along with warnings about draining people of their essence. But there was one article that made her frown deepen: 'Converting kids to the cause'. So, he was a normal, well-adjusted person, then.

There was one framed photograph on the tiled mantlepiece. It showed a young Hackett next to a bulldog in a dress, or possibly his mother. Propped up against it was his membership card to the Anti-Magic Party.

The detective returned from the bedroom and gestured to Fi that they could go. Outside the flat, Fi took a gulp of fresh air.

"Find anything in the bedroom?"

"Only that he folded his underwear. Come on, let's knock on some doors."

They knocked on the door opposite. An elderly man answered, leaning on a walking frame. Detective Ledd flashed his badge and asked about Hackett.

"He kept himself to himself really. We had to speak to him about his music when he first moved in, but he's kept it down since. The only time we heard him was when he told the kids off for kicking balls against the wall. He had a set of lungs on him then, for sure."

Other neighbours didn't even bother to answer their doors and Fi and Detective Ledd headed outside. A scrawny child with dirty brown hair sat next to Cressida.

Fi crouched down. "Do you like my familiar?"

The child nodded.

"She's lovely, isn't she?" Fi showed the child how to tickle Cressida behind her ears. "Do you live in these flats?"

The child nodded.

"Did you know Mr Hackett?"

His eyes narrowed. "He threatened to hit me and my brother if we didn't stop playing outside, but where else can we play? Mum won't let us down the park on our own."

"OK, well I don't think Mr Hackett will be coming back, so you don't worry about him anymore."

The child cheered up and raced inside, shouting to his brother about their change in fortunes.

The detective shook his head at Fi.

"What?"

He didn't bother to reply and instead studied his small notebook. "That's it for now, I'm going back to the station. Call me if you get any leads."

Fi resisted the urge to execute a sarcastic salute behind his back and gathered up Cressida for the long, hot walk home.

Two minutes later, she passed Finley on the street. He waved and crossed over to talk to her.

"Lovely day for a stroll."

"I suppose."

"Rumour is there's been another killing, at the school."

"How do you know that?" Fi's eyes narrowed and her magic sparked beneath her skin.

"It's all over town. The missus said that Brian at the Witch's Brew told Valerie, who told Sita, who told her."

Fi sighed. You couldn't stop gossip in a small town. "Where were you this morning?"

"Well, I dropped the boys at football practice on my way to the five a side match. I think there was a parents' brunch, but I was still in St Columba's for the away game. I scored the winning goal. So, is there a serial killer around then? What are the police doing?"

"You need three bodies for a serial killer." Years of watching true crime programmes sent the response to Fi's mouth without the implications of her words going through her brain. He took a step back and glanced around as if a killer could step out from behind a bush at any moment.

*That'll reassure him.*

"I mean, this is an ongoing investigation that I am not at liberty to discuss. Rest assured as soon as the police have anything they think the public should know, they'll make an announcement. I'd better go." With that, she dashed off, walking at double speed and leaving him staring after her on the pavement.

## Chapter 26

Fi stared at the text message on her phone.

*Report. In the next hour.*

Agent Jones didn't waste her words.

Fi sighed and reached out her hand to open the wooden door. The house responded before she could touch the handle, and the door swung open on its own. Fi smiled at the sentient building and gave it a pat as she walked inside.

"This came for you." Nell looked up from her Donkey Derby plans and pointed to a postcard on the table.

Fi grunted and mumbled something about needing to work. She read the postcard on the way upstairs.

*You got this! Trust your instincts, love Effie x*

The picture showed dozens of yachts bobbing on turquoise water in a harbour. Fi snorted. Effie might be psychic, but Fi did not feel like she got this.

In her room, Fi shut the door and pulled up the Magical Liaison Office profile on her computer while Cressida built a nest on her bed. She scrolled through the drive until she found a folder for reports. There was a template. That was good. She opened it. Clear headings shouted at her from the page. OK, so she just had to fill in each section. Fine.

She looked at the first section. Name of Officer. That was easy. Date of Incident. Yep. Description of Incident. Now she was flying. There were only so many words you could use to describe a dehydrated corpse.

She cut and paste that description into a second form for the teacher and linked the two together. Two related incident reports partly completed. Fi smiled with satisfaction.

*Could you keep that tapping down? Some of us are trying to sleep.*

"Sorry, Cress, I've got to fill out these incident reports."

*It's Cressida,* the golden wyrm grumbled and closed her emerald-green eyes.

Buoyed by her success at the start of the form, Fi's eyes raced ahead to the next section. Cause of Incident. Fi swore. That was the big unknown.

She flipped back to her personal profile and found her custom programme. It was a virtual cork board that replicated the ones in detective shows on TV. It helped Fi think and find connections. She typed what she knew into virtual post-its and positioned them on the board. She drew a thick red line between the two victims and typed the word 'exsanguinated'. She thought for a moment and added the name of the village to the board. That was about the only thing they had in common.

Except, possibly, they knew the killer. And they didn't seem to have many friends.

Fi huffed and did a quick search on the internet for Lucille Dankworth. She blinked as a youthful face came up. Fi clicked on it. An American actress with a birthdate less than twenty years ago who'd been in a couple of sitcoms. Not who she was looking for. She hadn't exactly expected the elderly lady to have a social media profile, but something would have been nice.

She tried Sam Hackett. He had a few more entries. One for the school where he worked; standard stuff about years of employment, blah, blah, blah. A private social media account…and links to an anti-magic group. A few clicks later, Fi was in a world of echo chamber chatrooms rife with anti-magic sentiment.

Hackett was prominent with the imaginative username Hackett86. Fi rolled her eyes. And his password was probably his birthday. Then she frowned. Why would someone so against magic work somewhere with supernatural protected status? There were more supernatural beings per capita in Omensford than in London. Weird.

Fi made a note of it on the corkboard, then copied it over into the Victim Background section of the form.

She bit her lip and added Finley to the list of potential suspects along with the next door neighbour. Fi checked out their social media profiles; nothing unusual. But then a murderer with links to blood magic wouldn't exactly advertise it. Both of them had kids, but did that make them more or less likely to be a killer?

She looked up the Omensford Old Boys football team and got pictures from the match earlier today. And there was Finley, scoring the only goal of the game. So, Finley's story checked out; there was no way he could have been in St Columba's for the match and made it back in time to kill Hackett after the kids' football practice. With a slump of her shoulders, she crossed him off the suspect list.

On a whim, she looked up Steve's social media page and saw pictures of a poached egg and avocado on toast and then a selfie of all the parents who had attended. There, at the back, was Lucille's neighbour; Eileen Chester. Fi swore. Her one remaining suspect now had an alibi for the second murder. She was about to cross the woman off her list, but…if Eileen had stayed behind after practice, maybe she could have killed the PE teacher and then made it to the brunch…

It was a long shot, but she didn't have any other theories. She kept Eileen's name on the board. Fi chewed on a chocolate bar as she thought. Both victims liked drinking at the pub, but the owner didn't get anything from killing them, in fact, he lost out because they'd run up tabs, and no one had mentioned any fights, if you didn't count Lucille walloping Harris for a comment about an inappropriate vegetable. She finished off her chocolate bar and let out a humph of despondency, the sugar not having its usual uplifting effect on her mood.

With no suspects, unless you counted any parent who disliked both a PE teacher and a cranky old woman, Fi went back to searching for blood magic. She got a few hits on some of the chatrooms that Hackett had frequented. She debated correcting some assumptions that all magic users needed blood for their spells but decided it was better not to get involved in the hate chat. She could channel her power to take out the chatroom's servers...She shook her head. It was too risky with her shaky control over her magic and it might blow up her trusty computer and then where would she be?

Her fingers hovered over the keyboard. Maybe she could hack the site and take it down with a denial of service attack...but then they'd find somewhere else to spew hate.

Fi sighed and copied over some of her research on blood magic. It wasn't much, but it filled up the report with a few more lines.

She typed out a reminder to speak to Maxi about getting her software onto the MLO drive. It would be so much easier, but she doubted she could just install it. Well, she could – their security was easy enough to bypass, especially since she had access to a login – but she shouldn't.

She saved the report down and hovered her cursor over the Submit icon. She had practically nothing to go on and no leads. But Agent Jones had demanded something.

Frustrated and wanting a distraction, she pulled back and focused on her magic, reaching out to sense other electricity. She saw the yellow white computer screen in front of her, and the small bundle of synapses that was Cressida curled up on the bed. She allowed her magic to flow further and it responded to her like a puppy, happy to play. Was that her mother's signature downstairs? With her mind, she followed a cable around the house, frowning at its unconventional set up. So that was what happened when a magical house added electricity.

Her phone buzzed. Fi yelped and her magic jumped. Above her, the bulb fizzed and shattered, raining glass onto the carpet. Cressida hissed. Fi sighed and checked the caller ID; Detective Ledd. She picked up.

"There hasn't been another murder has there?"

"Nope. Robbie's finished her tests on the body. He was drugged and it looks like it was the tea. Good job on finding the flask."

"Er, it was Cressida who found it…"

The small wyrm raised her head and Fi felt a warm contentment flood her chest, along with a smugness that didn't seem to belong to her.

"Well pass on my thanks. Anyway, thought you should know." The detective paused. "You haven't found any leads, have you? This is ugly and the brass are getting twitchy."

"I'm working on it, just about to submit a report actually."

"Good. That's…good. Send a copy over, will you?" Larry sounded relieved.

Fi mumbled something and he ended the call. Now she'd have to send in the report. She added a comment about the tea being drugged.

Why would someone do that? Either they knew Hackett well and didn't want him to suffer, or…maybe he was too tall for them to cut his throat. She noted that down too and pressed Submit.

A scream spiralled up the stairs.

## Chapter 27

Fi rushed down, Cressida at her heels, and they burst into the kitchen.

Agatha cradled Bea in her arms, rocking her from side to side. She looked up with tear-filled eyes. Fi froze.

"She collapsed. Oh goddess, she just collapsed! Look how pale she is!"

Fi knelt at her sister's side. "It's OK, we'll call an ambulance–"

"It's not natural, it's magic! Someone's taking her essence!" Nell crouched at her daughter's other side, stroking her granddaughter's hair.

Fi blinked in confusion. She couldn't feel anything supernatural, but she wasn't a nature witch. The most she could feel was electricity.

*Brimstone,* breathed Cressida.

Fi stood and pulled her hand through her white hair. "What? Are you sure?"

*Yes.*

"What is it? What's wrong with my baby?" Agatha stared at her sister.

"It's all connected. I just...I don't know how. It's alright, I'll call Agent Jones, they'll send a proper taskforce–"

Agatha passed Bea to Nell and stood. She marched over to Fi and grasped her by the shoulders.

"My baby – your niece – is in danger from someone who drains the blood from their victims, and you want to *wait* until a taskforce gets here?!"

"I..." Fi's head flopped back and forth as Agatha shook her shoulders.

"You need to get out there and stop this!"

"I don't know how!"

"Then figure it out! Look, look at this! She made this for you!" Agatha released Fi's shoulders and retrieved a piece of card from the table. She thrust it into Fi's hands. "Your niece believed in you, she thought you could do it. You're her bloody hero! Don't let her down."

Fi couldn't meet her sister's angry blue eyes. It was bad. Terrible enough that Agatha had used a curse word, even if it was a mild one. Fi stared down at the drawing in her trembling hands instead. It was a picture of her and Bea holding hands with a message; *Don't worry Aunty Fi, you can do it!*

Bea had drawn small hearts over the i's and a swirling design behind them. The background image caught Fi's eye. Her eyebrows drew together as she turned the paper, studying it. She moved to the kitchen table and leafed through more drawings. Each one had similar symbols drawn in bright colours; some in the background, others doodled over the paper. It reminded her of a Tri force but with more angles and strange curves that compelled her eyes to follow them. Her head jerked up. She had seen that symbol before.

Fi grabbed the papers and ran to the library.

"What is it? Where are you going?" Agatha called after her.

"I've been looking at everything wrong!"

## Chapter 28

Now Fi had a lead, she strode into the library, waving the papers. "I need books on demons."

The books fluttered their pages together.

"And I don't want any nonsense. This is life or death, and Bea is in trouble." She could feel the house sigh. She pointed to the symbol Bea had scribbled over and over. "That's right, your future owner is in danger. Now get me the book on demonology and anything else you can think of that might help me find these symbols."

A large book flew out of the bookshelf and landed on the coffee table with a thud.

"Thank you," Fi remembered to say, and she bent over the book and flicked through it as fast as she could. Not fast enough. The aged pages turned by themselves, quickly at first, then slower until the house's magic stopped. "Thank you," Fi whispered again.

She smoothed down Bea's drawings and compared them to the symbols on the page. She leaned back. It was a match.

She bent her head back down and read. It wasn't good. Brimstone! Why hadn't she connected the sulphurous smell with demons earlier? She shook her head in disbelief at her stupidity as her eyes travelled down the pages.

"What is it?" her mum asked quietly from the doorway.

"Demons." Fi pointed to the book. Nell approached and read over her shoulder. "I saw these symbols before. Someone's trying to bring a demon into our village."

"Just one person? I thought demon worshippers usually had a cult."

Fi snapped her fingers. "The children." Her mother's face creased with confusion. "Communing with a demon takes a lot of power. They're siphoning kids' energy instead of willing cultists. Look. They need the blood to feed the demon with a special knife and, once it's fed off three people and has drained enough energy from the kids, it'll be powerful enough to open a portal and get through. It's already killed two people…"

"Then we'd better stop whoever is channelling it before it kills a third."

"But how? The only connection between the two is that they live in the village, and neither were particularly well liked, especially by children. I think I know who's behind it, but I don't know where they'll strike next. And we can't afford to mess this up."

Nell pursed her lips as she thought. "And you can't feel any disturbances?"

"What do you mean?"

Nell sat next to her daughter. "Well, electricity is a form of energy, so I always wondered if your power wasn't only about electricity, if it was more energy related." Fi's mouth dropped open as her mother continued. "And if it is, then a portal to another realm is likely to cause a big disruption in energy fields, yes? So, are you sure you can't sense anything?"

"I'll try." Fi closed her eyes and concentrated. Cressida brushed against her legs, lending Fi a comforting warmth as the tech witch tapped into her power. She could feel the electricity running through the house and powering the lights, behind that, the faint magical hum of the sentient house itself was a background power that she ignored.

Fi took a breath and allowed her power to fill her, connecting with it instead of tamping it down. It crackled over her skin in waves, making her hair stand on end. She could sense fizzing electrical currents moving through her mother. She pushed her senses outwards.

A strong current in the kitchen must be Agatha, and, next to her, a fainter one; Bea. Fi reached out further, sweat beading on her forehead as she expanded her senses beyond the house. Her leg started to vibrate. A rhythmic buzz filled her ears, in time with the vibrations. Fi swore and answered her phone.

"Hello?"

"Fi, something's happening at the common." The familiar deep voice made her stomach sink. She rubbed her temples. A headache threatened; a dull ache on the knife edge of becoming a full migraine.

"What are you talking about, Mort?"

"I'm talking about a portal to another realm—"

"I'm on my way."

Fi hung up and headed out of the library. Cressida dogged her footsteps. She heard the swish of skirts and Nell was at her side.

"What are you doing? This is my responsibility."

Nell scoffed. "Someone is raising demons in my village and threatening our Donkey Derby. I think you'll find that, as Chair of the Omensford Witches', Wizards' and Warlocks' Institute, that makes it very much my responsibility. I'm coming with you. And that is that."

Fi stared at her mother, who swept past her with all the confidence of a senior witch. Fi had to jog to keep up as Nell strode through the kitchen, grabbed her broomstick from its place on the wall and headed out of the door.

Fi clutched the X-5000 and hurried after her mother. Halfway across the room, she paused and walked over to her sister, sat on the hard floor, cradling Bea's head in her lap. She bent over and planted a kiss on Bea's forehead. She started to stand, then placed a kiss on her sister's head.

"Don't worry. We're going to catch this bastard."

On the threshold, she paused again and touched the doorframe. "Keep them safe," she whispered to the house. Its shutters slammed shut and the doors locked behind her.

## Chapter 29

The witches raced to the common, their silhouettes dulled by the mounting clouds. Fi could feel the promise of rain in the air, and underneath that, the closeness that promised a summer storm. The mugginess pressed against her skin as they flew, pressing in on her as the air thickened around the common. Cressida sat bolt upright in front of her, her forked tongue darting out as if she could taste the air. Fi pulled her attention back to the ground.

On the common, white marquees and smaller tents were set up in a neat horseshoe shape around a marked oval racetrack for the donkeys. The animals huddled together in the middle of their makeshift pen, as if they knew something wasn't right.

Fi spotted a dark figure entering the gate. It kept to the treeline behind the tents, as if they didn't want to be spotted. Fi signalled to her mother and angled the X-5000 down. She cut off the power and landed behind the tall shadow with a soft thud. The tall figure turned, their face shadowed by the trees. A sword hung at their left hip – was that the special demon summoning knife? She held her hands out, gathering electricity to her palms.

"Halt!"

*Wait!*

The figure raised their arms until their hands were level with their head. Vines snaked out of the earth and pulled the figure to the ground. One of the vines clapped a leaf over their mouth.

"Mum! I had it handled!" Fi ignored the small wyrm and turned on her mother.

"I'm sure you did, dear, but with demons around, best to be safe than sorry. Now, shall we see who it is?"

Fi stepped forward and placed her hand on the figure's broad shoulder. She turned them towards her. With a groan, she pulled off the leaf that covered their mouth.

"Mort? What are you doing here?"

"I came to help." He smiled sheepishly.

*I told you to wait.*

The vines tightened.

"It's alright Mum, it's Mort."

"Oh, I'm terribly sorry." With a flick of her wrists, the vines disappeared back into the dry ground.

Mort rubbed his arm. "I told you on the phone; someone's trying to open a portal."

"How do you know that?"

"Er, well you know that I have some, er, ties with the underworld." Mort looked sheepish. Fi felt her heart squeeze;

he was adorable when he was contrite. She stamped down her emotions and nodded. She knew that he could somehow cross to the realm of the dead and he was a descendent of the god of death, or the god of death's assistant, or something. That was how they had got Effie back after her sister had killed her.

"Right, well, my family doesn't only guard the gates to the underworld, we also monitor the gates to the other realms...and one of them is pressing against the fabric of reality over there."

"By other realms you mean..."

"The demon realm. Among others."

"So...hell?"

Mort sighed but he didn't argue. "In layman's terms, yes, you could call it that. It's certainly nothing good."

"OK, so how do we stop it?"

"Well, demons usually possess people and force them to do their bidding, in exchange for granting a wish and they need a lot of energy, from cultists normally–"

Fi shook her head and interrupted him. "They're draining energy from village kids, not cultists."

Mort's face was grim. "For a demon to assume a corporeal form in our realm, energy isn't enough. They require blood – human sacrifice..."

"They've had two of those already. Why didn't you say something after Lucille was killed?"

"I wasn't sure until the second body, and I couldn't pinpoint where it was happening until I called you. I still don't know who the vessel is!"

"Vessel?"

Nell nodded briskly, her eyes scanning the common. "The person who communes with the demon and typically agrees to be possessed. If you can feel a portal, they must be close."

"But I can't understand why they're opening the portal here. There're only the donkeys, and they won't work as a sacrifice…"

"Alf!" Nell sprinted across the dried grass in her sensible shoes, heading towards the colourful caravan.

Fi met Mort's eyes and they ran after the witch.

"We've got to stop whoever it is from killing their third victim. If the demon can assume its own form, it'll be practically unstoppable."

## Chapter 30

A body sprawled on the white steps leading up to the caravan. A figure in a long robe stood over it, hands raised to the cloudy sky. At their neck, a pendant glistened in the dim light. Nell loosed a bolt of green magic at the figure, knocking it backwards onto the hard ground.

Nell bent over the body. "No, no, no, no. Oh, Alf."

Fi skidded to a halt next to her mother. Her eyes widened as she stared down. Alf's throat had been cut, and there were slashes on his forearms – it looked like he'd put up a fight. He gasped up, his eyes desperately trying to focus on Nell.

Mort knelt by his side and applied pressure to the wound, trying to staunch the bleeding. As the blood left Alf's body, it defied gravity and beaded up to join the bronzed knife that the hooded figure gripped, now standing upright and panting.

Above the figure, a dark shape hovered with glowing red eyes. Its silhouette was becoming clearer and clearer as it fed on Alf's life force. Strange clouds moved in circular motions behind it, joining with the mounting storm in murky patterns.

"We can't let the demon drain the blood!"

"It's already here!"

"No." Mort shook his head. "That's its spirit, but if the portal forms, it'll come through."

Fi pounded her head, trying to think. "Get him out of here. Maybe if he's far enough away, his blood won't feed it."

Mort lifted the old man easily in his arms.

"Wait!" Nell moved her hands in a complicated motion over his throat, making a ward. The blood hit an invisible barrier and trickled back down, like it had hit a pane of glass. "Now, go!"

"No! What are you doing?!" The figure shrieked with a woman's voice, stepping forward. "You can't break the connection!"

*We are so close.* A rumbling voice rolled around the common.

Fi shivered. Somehow the voice conveyed power, darkness and the promise of pain in one horrifying package. Fi gathered her power. Control, remember control. She let loose a bolt of electricity at the robed figure, judging the force so that it wouldn't be fatal. She hoped.

The figure screamed and fell to the ground, her hood falling down from her face. Fi stepped forward and stopped.

Lying on the ground was the Magic Club leader – White Hare, no, Rabbit. "Valerie?" Fi's heart sank. She was right. The woman had aligned herself with a demon and using innocent children to bring it into the world.

"You don't know what you're doing! I need to protect the children!" Valerie scrambled to her feet, her eyes wide, pleading.

"Protect them? You're killing people!"

"You don't understand. They were horrible to the children. Childhood is meant to be a time of wonder and joy, and they were hurting them."

And the dots connected in Fi's mind. The old woman who shouted at children and stopped them from playing in the park. The teacher who insulted kids and threw dodgeballs at them.

"But why Alf? Children love riding the donkeys." Fi's brow furrowed with confusion.

"He was mean. He wouldn't let them ride. He didn't keep them safe." Valerie's voice held an echo of something unnatural.

"Is that what you think or what the demon you've sold your soul to is telling you to think?"

The club leader grabbed her head. "No, no, he's helping me to protect them. I just want all the children to be safe and happy. He promised they'd be safe."

"If that thing comes through to this realm, everyone will be in danger. Including the children! Your magic club kids are dying now."

*No! She lies with the forked tongue of a serpent.* The voice echoed around the common, conjuring images of slime and darkness and the thick stench of brimstone. *Help me and I shall keep them safe. I only need one more...There!*

Valerie revolved slowly to face the caravan. On the steps stood Young Alf, staring up at the demonic cloud overhead.

"Where's Da?"

## Chapter 31

There was one horrible moment where Fi looked from Young Alf to Valerie as Young Alf's eyes moved from Valerie to Fi. Valerie stared hungrily at the teenager, standing bemused on the steps. Her face shadowed with something inhuman that lengthened her teeth and slitted her irises.

*Now!* roared the demon.

Valerie lunged forward, the ancient knife in her hand glinting in the fading light. Fi threw herself at the club leader, knocking them both to the dry ground.

"Run!" she shouted to Young Alf through a cloud of dust.

The boy stared at them with wide eyes before he sprinted to the donkey enclosure. Valerie bucked her hips and sent Fi flying. The tech witch rolled onto the hard ground and pushed herself up. Valerie's eyes fixed on the boy. Fi groaned. He was trying to free the donkeys.

Valerie made to run to him, but Cressida twined between her ankles and tripped the woman onto the floor.

"Nice job," Fi grunted to the small wyrm as she crawled over to the prone woman. Cressida yelped as the club leader kicked her in the head. Valerie swiped wildly with the knife. Fi recoiled as if she'd felt the blow. Then, the witch crabwalked backwards on her hands and feet to avoid the sharp blade.

"This is the only way! The only way I can keep them all safe!"

"Alf is a child! You don't want to kill him!"

Valerie shook her head. "It is one boy, one boy to save many." The demon's voice rolled around her words in a hollow echo.

"That's the demon talking, not you!"

Valerie met Fi's gaze and, for an instant, her eyes flashed the deep, living red of a lava flow. "We are one and the same."

The club leader scrambled upright. Fi was right behind her. Valerie turned her back on the witch, hunting the boy. Fi's chest heaved with anger. She gathered her power to her hands and launched a ball of blue electricity at the middle-aged woman.

A thick tendril of cloud whipped down from the demonic shape hovering above the club leader. Fi's power crackled against it and fizzed out. Valerie turned and glared at the witch.

Behind her, Young Alf swatted donkeys on their rumps, desperately trying to make the stubborn creatures leave their pen.

Fi channelled her power into palms again. "I won't stop. I won't let you kill him, so you'll have to go through me first."

Valerie's smile was enough to chill a hardened warrior. Her eyes flashed red again as the demon took hold. Above her, the smoky cloud seemed to smile too. "With pleasure, after all, it does not matter who's blood powers us."

## Chapter 32

Valerie ran at Fi. The witch loosed bolts of electricity at the magic club leader. With superhuman, or, more accurately, demonic reflexes, Valerie dodged left and right, avoiding the crackling balls of power. Behind her, one collided with the refreshments tent in an explosion of sparks.

Fi feinted, pretending to aim left and changing direction at the last second as Valerie darted right. The electricity crashed into Valerie. She stopped dead with the force of the impact. The tendril of smoky cloud snaked down again. The electricity fizzed around it and sucked into the air, adding to the close sticky feeling of the coming storm.

*What interesting power thee has...*

Fi's hair stood out wildly around her head thanks to the charge that accompanied her magic. "Do you want another taste?"

She let loose a stream of lightning into the cloud. The demon laughed. It sounded like a saw rasping against wood.

*What are you doing? Why are you fighting a cloud?!* Cressida hissed.

Fi stared at the wyrm. "You're right."

*Of course I am!* Cressida shook her head back and forth as if it were unthinkable that she could ever be wrong.

Fi adjusted her stance and squared her shoulders with all the confidence that came from one combat training session with a harpy.

Valerie lunged forward, swiping with the knife. Fi dodged the first cut and struck out with her fist. But Valerie, aided by the demon, was too quick. She sidestepped neatly and circled around the witch, waiting for an opening.

Fi kept her guard up, like she'd been taught. She ran through the instructions in her mind; distract them, fight dirty, fight any way you can to get them down and stay safe.

With a burst of inspiration, Fi forced her eyes wide and pointed to the other side of the common. The demon followed her finger and Valerie turned with him. Fi ran forward and jumped onto Valerie's back.

The woman span in a circle, trying to dislodge Fi.

*What was your plan here?* Cressida's voice sounded in her mind.

Fi grunted, clinging on as Valerie thrashed beneath her. The wyrm sighed and sank her sharp teeth into Valerie's calf. The woman screamed and bent forward, sending Fi flying over her. The witch landed on the ground. Hard.

Valerie panted, gripping her calf with her hands. The knife was on the floor. Fi and Valerie realised this at the same time and both scrambled for the blade. Fi grabbed Valerie's ankle and yanked her backwards.

Valerie turned and kicked out at the witch. Fi dodged the foot and crawled forward until she was on top of the woman. She closed her fist and punched Valerie in the face. There was a crunch.

Valerie screamed. "My nose!"

"Ah!" Fi shook her hand. No one had mentioned how much it would hurt to punch someone. Fi's jaw dropped. The blood leaking from Valerie's nose pooled on her lip and then began to flow to the blade. As the blood touched the surface, a symbol – the mirror of the one on the woman's necklace – glowed a deep, swirling red. Power surged towards the demonic cloud.

"No!" Valerie realised what was happening. She tried to staunch the bleeding with her hands, but the blood trickled through her fingers.

*I am sorry to lose thee, my vessel, but it is for the greater good...*

## Chapter 33

With a sob, Valerie released her hands and lay them by her side. She closed her eyes.

"No!" Fi pressed her palms over Valerie's bleeding nose, futilely trying to stop the blood seeping up.

The leader's eyes opened. A look of triumph flickered across her face. And Fi felt a blade cut across her arm.

Fi cried out. Valerie's smile widened maniacally. The blood beaded on the witch's arm. Fi watched in horror as the bead grew and then flew to the demonic blade.

*Yes! Well done, little one, thee shall be richly rewarded when I enter this realm.*

Behind the demon, the clouds shifted and crackled together in a swirling vortex of black and crimson. The air chilled and the hairs on Fi's neck pricked upright.

She stared, helpless, as the blood flowed from her arm towards the glowing bronze knife.

*You have to stop this!* Cressida whined as she paced back and forth next to the witch.

"I can't…I don't know…"

*Well, figure it out, because I'm not losing you, too!*

Fi reached out her uninjured arm to stroke the small, golden wyrm. She could feel her life force slipping away as the demon pulled the blood from her body. So, this is how it happens, she thought. Bled dry by a demon while a wyrm watches.

Valerie pushed her backwards and Fi let it happen. What was the point of fighting? There was nothing she could do. Cressida curled around her neck and nuzzled her chin. Reassuring warmth filled Fi's heart and she let it in. What was the point in living a life without closeness? Why did she fight her emotions so much? Her eyes filled with tears as she reached out to stroke her familiar.

The club leader turned to the portal and raised her arms. "Yes, we are so close!"

Mort stepped up behind Valerie, sword in hand. He wrapped one arm around the woman and crushed her to him. He looked at Fi.

"What are you doing?" Fi's face creased in confusion and her head swam. She must have lost more blood than she thought. Mort was here. Did that mean Alf was dead? But the demon wasn't yet in this realm. Her head pulsed.

"There's still time. She's the vessel. If I kill her, it will break the connection with the demon and the kids. It will stop all of this."

His face hardened. He raised the sword to bring it across Valerie's throat. The blade glowed with an otherworldly purplish white over a black so deep that it seemed to suck everything to it. He would kill her, Fi knew it with a strange certainty and she could see the concern and pain on his face. He was a doctor, even if he was allied to the God of Death. This wasn't right. She couldn't let him take on this burden, not when she could stop it.

"Wait!" Fi forced herself to her feet. "I can stop her."

## Chapter 34

Mort looked at Fi, then nodded. He lowered his sword. Fi's heart swelled at the trust he gave her as he released the woman, but he stood close and kept the blade in his hand, ready to step in if she failed.

Valerie sneered. The demon laughed. Fi felt the blood flow faster from her wound. She ignored it. Instead, she focused. She closed her eyes and inhaled. Power flowed through her body. She reached out with her senses.

There was Cressida's crackling heartbeat and her synapses shone like a golden firework. Fi reached further. Behind her, the dull electrical signals from the donkeys pulsed with fear and adrenaline. A human, that must have been Young Alf, stood next to a stubborn, unmoving ass.

And in front, she found Mort's energy signature. He sparked with something she couldn't place; a light both bright and yet dark, hot and yet cold, at the same time. She forced her magic on to the duller, more human electricity inside Valerie.

And above them all, the growing energy of the demon shadow. Fi kept her eyes shut and concentrated on Valerie. She felt every electrical pulse in the woman's body. She followed them to the synapses that connected in her brain. It was like watching a light show in pulses of sparking energy.

Fi took another breath. And with a snap of her fingers, she cut off the electricity in Valerie's brain. She opened her eyes. The club leader sank to the ground, the blade falling to the dry dirt with a clunk. The first rain drops fell from the sky, cutting through the demonic cloud.

*What hath thee done?* the demon roared.

Fi glanced down at her arm. The blood dripped out of the cut at a normal speed, trickling down her arm and pooling onto the ground, merging with the rain. Fi swayed in the cool precipitation.

The portal shrank as the demon cursed them all. It bobbed above its comatose vessel in confused chaos. Then it narrowed its red eyes, shrieked out in fury and dived for Fi. She held her arms up against the grey cloud, but in its insubstantial form, it flowed around her, surrounding her with darkness and those demonic eyes, before racing across the field.

"Is it gone?" she asked Mort.

He looked round. The portal winked shut as if it had never existed. He nodded.

Fi staggered to Valerie. She took hold of the woman's soft hand, squeezed and used her power to restart Valerie's synapses. The magic club leader blinked, and Fi let out the breath she hadn't realised she was holding.

"What happened?"

"You were possessed by a demon and killed three people."

Valerie winced and shrank back, hugging her knees to her chest. In hindsight, maybe Fi should have sugar-coated it a bit, but the woman had welcomed a demon into this realm and tried to kill her, so Fi didn't have a lot of sympathy left.

"Two people," Mort said. Both women looked at him. He coughed. "Alf was still alive when the ambulance arrived, so you've only killed…two people…"

Fi could have hugged him. But there was a demonic vessel between them, so instead she settled for a smile as she tucked her frizzy hair back into its ponytail, ignoring the bloodstains that smeared across her clothes.

*Don't you ever do that to me again!*

Fi stroked the small wyrm, still curled around her throat. "Aw, Cress, I didn't know you cared so much."

*Of course I do! And don't call me Cress.* The wyrm snapped at Fi's fingers.

Detective Ledd sprinted across the field, his suit jacket waving in the wind like an unlikely cape. "Reports of a disturbance and I find you…" He skidded to a halt and spun slowly, taking in the smoking refreshments tent, the fleeing donkeys and the blood running down Fi's arm. "Well, well, well, what's gone on here then?"

Fi and Mort filled him in. The detective's eyes got wider and wider until they boggled almost out of his head when Fi mentioned the portal. To his credit, the first thing he said after they had finished was; "Valerie Blanc a.k.a White Rabbit, you are under arrest for the murder of Lucille Dankworth and Sam Hackett…"

Fi and Mort stood to one side while the detective finished his arrest and walked a handcuffed Valerie to his car.

"So…"

"So…"

Fi wanted to say something to make things right with Mort. She opened her mouth, but red and yellow lights sparked across her vision. She blinked and swayed. She felt herself start to fall. Then she was in his arms, staring up at him.

"We should get you to a doctor."

"You are a doctor." Fi started to giggle. He gave her a lopsided smile and laughed.

He smoothed a strand of hair behind her ear. She stopped giggling and gazed into his chocolate brown eyes. Raindrops fell around them, slowly at first then faster as the clouds burst. The soft earthy smell of fresh rain on a summer's day rose from the ground, with, yes, a tint of brimstone. He bent his head towards her. She ran the tip of her tongue over her lips. This was it. They were going to kiss. While sober. She closed her eyes.

"'Ere, there's something wrong with this donkey." Young Alf called from across the field.

Fi huffed out a sigh. That was about right.

# Epilogue

"Five pounds on Burrito for the next race." Fi handed over her money in the betting tent.

"Are you sure?" Liv looked at the small donkey with the tan spot dubiously. He nibbled the grass, unaware of the two witches watching him. "He hasn't moved all day."

"You bet your ass I am!" Fi laughed. Inside her head, she could hear Cressida's groan. "I'm feeling lucky."

Liv took the money and handed Fi a betting slip and a leaflet with the race order for the day. Fi smiled and meandered over to the refreshments tent, clutching her betting slip and the letter. The rain had continued overnight, and the ground was soft underfoot. The air felt cleaner, too, as if the rain had washed away the mugginess that came with too much heat and the oppressiveness of a demon stalking the town.

The WWWI members had scrubbed the field of any demonic residue and there were no signs of the fight or the danger that the small town had faced. With the sun peeking out from behind cotton clouds, the day was fresh. The perfect time for new beginnings.

Inside the tent, she ordered a can of diet cola and a sparkling water for the wyrm and asked Steve if she could have a word. The werewolf made his excuses and joined her in a quiet corner of the marquee. He handed over the can and the water. Fi opened the water first and poured it into a small dish that she dug out of her pocket. Cressida lapped the cold water with messy enjoyment.

Fi smiled and opened her can, enjoying the metallic hiss that promised cool, bubbly refreshment.

"This came for you today." Fi handed over the letter, watching Steve carefully as he opened it. Curiosity overcame her, so she started babbling. "It was with a postcard from Effie. She's having a great time in Italy. I think her next stop'll be Greece."

Fi stopped talking and watched Steve. The postcard had been brief: *I knew you could do it, Fi! Nell – don't worry, Alf will be fine. PS give the letter to Steve.*

"Oh goodness." Steve sank into a wooden chair.

Fi pulled up her own folding chair. "Is it bad news?" She was such an idiot. It had never occurred to her that it would be bad news, she had been so eager to find out what the letter said.

"It's from Effie…"

"And?"

Steve looked up, his eyes wide and glassy. "She wants me to run her café when it reopens." He tapped the letter. "It says the structural work should be done soon, then she needs me to redecorate and refurbish. What am I going to do, Fi? I'll have to talk to Glen. I haven't worked in years, not since we had Zadie… What am I going to do?"

"Hey," Fi placed a hand on his arm. "This is a good thing. Effie wouldn't ask you to do something you couldn't handle, and you already baked for her, before her shop burned down, and I know you make a mean cup of tea. It'll be great, you'll see."

"I'm glad you think so…because she says you'll help."

"What?!"

Steve handed over the letter and pointed to the last paragraph. Effie had indeed promised that Fi would be on hand to help out…and bake scones. Typical Effie, Fi thought, and, of course she knew that Fi wouldn't say no.

"She says she'll be back for the opening; she wants it to be on Halloween! I've got to talk to Glen!" Steve stood up abruptly, knocking over the folding chair. "Sorry," he mumbled as he set it upright, started to leave, then turned back to Fi and enveloped her in a huge hug. Fi patted his back awkwardly. He released her, gave her a beaming grin and pushed his glasses back up his nose before heading out of the tent.

Fi sat back against the chair and took a sip of her drink, enjoying the artificial taste of the sweeteners mixed with the bubbles.

"Aunty Fi! Aunty Fi!"

Fi waved to her niece, who ran over to her. Agatha followed behind with Neville, balancing cakes and cups of tea in her hands.

"How are you feeling, bumble Bea?"

"Good. I don't know why I had to go to the doctors." Bea stopped to give her mother a look that belonged on a teenager rather than a seven-year-old. Agatha rolled her eyes behind her daughter's back. The girl, and all the children in the magic club, had regained consciousness at the same time that Fi had knocked out Valerie. Mort had rushed around Omensford, checking temperatures and other vital signs while an ambulance whisked Fi away for a check-up.

"But, guess what?" her niece continued, stroking Cressida, who purred happily before returning to her water dish.

"What?"

"I got to ride on a donkey! Dad took a picture – Dad, show Aunty Fi!"

Neville dutifully took out his phone and swiped through twenty pictures of Bea sitting happily astride a donkey as Young Alf walked it around the makeshift racecourse.

The speakers crackled into life and Nell's familiar voice boomed across the field. "All riders for the three p.m race, please make your way to the racetrack. And remember, we need your consent forms back at the betting tent or you will not be able to race.

"I'd like to thank the Loupin Antique Shop for sponsoring this race." Glen gave a wolfish smile as he stood next to Nell, who went onto list the names of the riders and the donkeys taking part in the race. Steve hopped from foot to foot off to one side, letter in hand.

"And thank you to everyone who has given donations for a care package for Alf, without whom we would not have the Donkey Derby at all. We also have a card for you to sign. If you want to contribute or sign the card, please speak to Liv in the betting tent. I will be delivering the package to the hospital after the races, so get any donations in soon."

In the background, the church clock chimed three times.

"Riders, to your places!"

Fi joined the crowd vying for a good viewing spot as the children, who all met the age requirement and had handed in the appropriate waivers, strapped on their helmets and mounted their donkeys. Young Alf stood next to the starting line. This was the third race of the day, and he was into his stride as race starter.

At a nod from Nell, he gave a piercing whistle, and the donkeys set off. Number six ambled forward and started to graze as her rider made encouraging noises to get her to go forward. Number three stopped abruptly halfway around the track, sending his rider over his head and onto the grass.

The others raced on, in the closest stride to a canter that donkeys can do.

"And it's Number four by a nose! Congratulations to Burrito and their rider, Zadie Loupin!"

"Yes!" Fi shouted, punching her fist into the air. She turned and collided with a man's chest.

"You seem happy."

Fi looked up and up, until she met Mort's chocolate brown eyes. They sparkled with laughter.

"I just won big on the races."

"Drinks on you then."

Fi nodded.

"How's your arm?" Mort reached for her bandaged forearm.

"Fine, it's fine. I'm fine."

*Tell him you want to be with him. It's so obvious.*

She glared at the small wyrm and fidgeted with her hands, then decided to go for it. She grabbed Mort's hand and pulled him to the edge of the field, trying to ignore the pleasant pulse of heat that spiralled through her arm and lodged itself in her stomach. Once they were out of the throng of people, she stopped and turned to him.

"Look…"

"It's OK, you don't have to say anything."

Fi opened her mouth, then closed it again. He was giving her an out. But she didn't want one, she wanted to see if this thing between them could be something more. A sudden lightness filled her chest. She wanted more. Her lips curved into a slow, playful smile.

"You still owe me."

He frowned in confusion.

"For going to the Spring Social with you."

Mort smiled. "So I do."

"And I promised to teach you how to play videogames."

"So you did."

"So…do you want to come over and play something?"

Mort pretended to think, before grinning even wider. "Sounds like a date."

Fi flushed and bounced on her feet.

"Shall we go now? While everyone's occupied?" he offered.

Fi glanced back at the racetrack. Glen and Steve had hoisted Zadie up onto their shoulders and were walking her around the course in a victory lap while the donkeys stared in the nonchalant way of all donkeys as they decided whether to kick out or continue eating.

Her mother's voice came over the speakers again. "If everyone could gather in the far left corner of the field, our broomstick display team is ready for the crisp drop." A cheer sounded across the field and all the children raced over to the orange markers where the crisp packets would fall.

"Sure, just give me a minute. There's something I've got to do. Why don't you collect my winnings and get us a couple of cans?" She handed Mort her betting slip and watched him step into a tent.

She sighed – a soppy sound that belonged on her sister's lips rather than hers – and fought to wipe the grin off her face. When she was sure that she was in control of her giddy emotions, Fi squared her shoulders and walked over to a pen where a donkey stood alone, tied to a post with enchanted rope.

Cressida hissed as they approached and hopped down, refusing to enter the invisible ward that the entire WWWI had banded together to create.

"So, are you going to talk yet?"

The donkey huffed. Its eyes glowed a deep red.

*You're wasting your time,* the small wyrm huffed.

"Look, I know you're in there. So, you can talk to me, or I can hand you over to the Magical Liaison Office, who are very interested in demons." She tapped her cheek with one finger. "Or there's a lot of kids hyped up on sugar who want to ride a donkey… So, let's try again; what's your name?"

"Thy mortal tongue couldst not pronounce my name," the donkey answered with a level of disdain that matched its long face. He paused and then spoke again, "But…thou may call me Timaeus."

Fi snorted out a laugh. "Really? Your name is Tim-ey-ass?!"

The donkey glared at her, but Fi couldn't help it. She bent over, hooting with laughter.

# Thank you

A special thank you to my amazing patreon: Emma Ward who always supports me.

If you want to support Gemma, you can find her on [www.patreon.com/G_Clatworthy](www.patreon.com/G_Clatworthy) for exclusive first reads of new stories.

You can also join her newsletter for at [www.gemmaclatworthy.com](www.gemmaclatworthy.com) for a [free prequel](free prequel) to her Rise of Dragons series and a free short story based on one of the Omensford witches. You can follow Gemma on [www.instagram.com/gemmaclatworthy](www.instagram.com/gemmaclatworthy), [www.facebook.com/gemmaclatworthy](www.facebook.com/gemmaclatworthy) or join the Facebook reader's group [Gemma's book wyrms.](Gemma's book wyrms.)

# Other Books by G Clatworthy

Books in the Rise of the Dragons series:

Awakening

Solstice of Dragons

Equinox Betrayal

Darkest Deception

Attack on Avalon

Fated Bloodlines

Books in the Omensford series (set in the Rise of the Dragons universe):

Bedsocks and Broomsticks

Cream Teas and Crystal Balls

Donkeys and Demons

Pumpkins and Popstars

# Children's Books

### The Child Who series:

The Girl Who Lost Her Listening Ears

The Boy Who Lost His Listening Ears

The Girl Who Dreamed of Sleep

The Boy Who Dreamed of Sleep

### Nanny Pastry series:

Nanny Pastry and the Nimble Ninjabread Man

### Other books:

Coronavirus in the words of children

## About the Author

Gemma started writing during the 2020 lockdown and loves fantasy fiction and dragons in particular. She lives in Wiltshire with her family and two cats and also enjoys crafts of all kinds. You can see all her writing on [www.patreon.com/G_Clatworthy](www.patreon.com/G_Clatworthy). Join the conversation at [Gemma's book wyrms](Gemma's book wyrms) readers' group on Facebook.

She also writes children's books. You can find out more on her website [www.gemmaclatworthy.com](www.gemmaclatworthy.com) or follow her on Instagram ([www.instagram.com/gemmaclatworthy](www.instagram.com/gemmaclatworthy)) or Facebook ([www.facebook.com/gemmaclatworthy](www.facebook.com/gemmaclatworthy)).

Made in the USA
Columbia, SC
25 May 2023